Deal with a Ghost

Marilyn Singer

DEAL
with
a
GHOST

Henry Holt and Company ▪ New York

Thanks to: Steve Aronson, Andrea Cascardi, Kathleen Cotter, Taifa Graves, Matt Rosen, the staff of Henry Holt, Asher Williams, and, especially, Lauri London and Simone Kaplan.

Henry Holt and Company, Inc.
Publishers since 1866
115 West 18th Street
New York, New York 10011

Henry Holt is a registered
trademark of Henry Holt and Company, Inc.

Published in Canada by Fitzhenry & Whiteside Ltd.,
195 Allstate Parkway, Markham, Ontario L3R 4T8.

Library of Congress Cataloging-in-Publication Data
Singer, Marilyn.
Deal with a ghost / Marilyn Singer.
p.   cm.
Summary: Sixteen-year-old Delia is more eager to play a
manipulative dating game than to adapt to her new school, but
then she finds that she has a personal connection to the ghost
said to be haunting the school.
[1. Ghosts—Fiction.   2. High schools—Fiction.   3. Schools—Fiction.]   I. Title.
PZ7.S6172De   1997   [Fic]—dc20   96-42994

ISBN 0-8050-4797-2
First Edition—1997
Printed in the United States of America on acid-free paper. ∞
1   3   5   7   9   10   8   6   4   2

To Laura Aronson

Deal with a Ghost

chapter one

———

"So, how does it feel to be going to a haunted school?"

Deal jumped and whirled around. A boy was standing there. That wasn't good. And it wasn't like her. From the time she was little she'd learned to watch her back. But she'd let the new school, dim and hulking as an old fortress, confuse her, and so the boy had managed to slip past her guard.

She recovered quickly, though, slowly rolling her shoulders as if her startled spin had been nothing more than an adjustment of her backpack. Then, deliberately, coolly, she looked the boy up and down. Medium height, medium weight, neutral clothes, brown hair, brown eyes, minor zits. Acceptable looking, really. But even if Deal had been in the mood for a flirtation, which she wasn't, this kid wasn't her type. He was panting. The bell hadn't rung yet. There wasn't a fire. So the only explanation for the huffing and puffing was that, like an eager puppy, he'd hurried to catch up to her and hand her his little line. Deal was not interested in eager.

Still, she wouldn't snub him outright. You never know when somebody like him might come in handy for something, she thought. "All schools are haunted," she replied with a yawn.

The boy looked puzzled. "What do you mean?" he asked.

Eager *and* inept, she thought. Usually when she made that sort of cryptic remark, which she often did, the Tom, Dick, or Fred she was talking to would wink or nod or knowingly smile, as though he was sharing a private joke with her, or because he wanted her to know he thought she was smart, which made him smart, too, for appreciating it. Sometimes he'd add, "Yeah, I get what you mean," whether he did or not. It was part of the Dating Game (or, as Deal referred to it, the *Baiting* Game). This puppy not only couldn't play the Game, he hadn't even read the manual. And he didn't have a clue that he was facing a master.

Well, that was okay. She'd made a fine art of the Game. Played it better than anyone else around. But lately she'd gotten tired of it. There were other ways to get through life, weren't there?

The kid was still waiting for an answer. He looked so earnest that Deal took pity on him and explained, "All schools are full of ghosts. Sitting in the classrooms, wandering the halls, smoking in the john. Who could forget

Jimmy Jones and his Hail Mary pass that saved the big game? Or Susie Smith, remember her? The most beautiful homecoming queen who ever lived? How about Johnny, Jerry, Joey, those wild and crazy guys who put the stink bomb in the supply closet or the auditorium or Mr. Teacher Man's car and everybody's still talking about it to this day. Look . . ." She pointed to a display case they were standing next to. It was filled with photos and trophies of past winning basketball teams. "Ghosts," she said.

"Very poetic," the boy said with a smile.

Deal squinted to see if he was mocking her, which would have raised him a notch in her estimation. But he wasn't. She shrugged and began to amble away, hoping she was headed in the right direction.

The boy followed. "But I'm talking about real ghosts. Or *ghost*. There's only one—but she's a doozy. Weeps, wails, dresses in white, the whole bit."

"Really? You've seen her?" Deal asked, mildly interested.

"Well, not exactly. But Al Benson did and he told me."

"Who's Al Benson?"

"The custodial engineer."

"You mean the janitor," said Deal, stepping squarely on someone's old math test, which had apparently survived Mr. Benson's cleanup, and leaving a perfect and complete footprint.

"They were going to close this place, y'know." The

boy gestured around him. "Too old and shabby and over-crowded. A real relic, they said."

"Yes, I know," Deal replied. Gram had told her, even provided a photo of the school board's new twenty-million-dollar pride and joy, James E. Brooks High School, in the "information packet" she'd sent before her granddaughter was, as Deal put it, "dumped in Gram's lap." The packet also contained Gram's house rules, of which there were fifteen, school registration forms for Deal's mother, Renee, to sign, and a key to the house in case Gram wasn't there to let Deal in when she arrived. She wasn't.

"The new school—Brooks—first it was supposed to open in September. But it wasn't quite finished. They were going to postpone the opening till next fall, but the parents complained. So they said okay, then how about for spring term? They figured they'd hustle over the records and all those piles of paper during Christmas break and give everybody a Happy New Year," said the kid.

"Yes, I know," Deal repeated, glancing around. The corridor had been steadily growing more and more crowded as they walked, with knots of kids talking, joking, exchanging books, cigarettes, photos, stories. It was all so familiar—and so alien. Something Deal was part of and apart from. Maybe this is how the world looks to a ghost, she thought. In which case this woman in white and I have something in common. She choked off a laugh.

The boy didn't notice. He was still babbling on about the new high school. "They had every type of engineer with every type of credential you can think of working on that place. The joint had more inspections than a meat-packing plant. So, what happened?"

"They decided to test the boiler and, overnight, the basement blew up," Deal replied.

"Right," said the boy, undeterred by the fact that she'd already known the punch line. "Good thing nobody was hurt, or Brooks would be haunted, too. And so here we are, back at the good old relic, Blain Schott—affectionately known as Brain Rot—High." He grinned. He had a gap between his front teeth like the guy on the cover of *Mad* magazine. It made Deal involuntarily grin back.

Then a group of guys brushed past her. "Hey, who's the new babe?" she heard one of them say. She gave him a discreet sideways glance, but all she could see was one meaty arm and half a sweatshirt. She turned her head in the other direction. Three girls were eyeing her curiously. They looked away when she caught their glance.

All of a sudden, Deal's chest felt tight. She needed to be alone. "Thanks for the report," she told the boy dismissively and squinted down the hall, searching for a girls' room.

"It's three doors down," the boy said.

"What is?"

"The girls' room. Isn't that what you're looking for?"

Deal was startled and annoyed. She hadn't thought she'd been so obvious. "No, I'm not," she nearly snapped. Watch it, girl. Relax, she told herself. Remember the three C's—Cool, Calm, and Chronically Clever.

The boy cocked his head. "You must feel weird being here, starting a new school in the middle of the year. You must miss your friends," he said, sounding genuinely concerned.

It made Deal uncomfortable. "I can live without them," she said nonchalantly. I can live without any-body, she declared silently. Including you, Renee.

Then the bell rang. Damn, Deal swore to herself. Consulting the white slip of paper in her hand, she stepped up her amble to a stride, thinking to shake the eager puppy at last.

But the boy kept pace with her. "I say, I say," he said, reading over her shoulder. "What a co-inky-dink."

"What?" Deal laughed in spite of herself. Nobody on earth talked like that. This kid must be broadcasting from Neptune.

"Five-thirteen. It's my homeroom, too," he explained.

"Great," Deal muttered.

"It's this way." He led her to the room and held open the door for her.

Five-thirteen was the music room. It was dominated by a large black piano, which Deal could see through the doorway. One glance at it and she felt herself relax. Pianos always calmed her—like lakes, overstuffed sofas, and thick ceramic bowls full of tomato soup, the things she'd miss from home. She rolled her shoulders again and sauntered into the room.

Hardly anyone was there yet, so she had her choice of seats. She picked one near the door that would let her both read her astrology book and watch the people filing in. Four preppy girls bounced into the classroom first like they belonged there, followed by a slinking leather-and-studs trio, only two of whom seemed comfortable in their clothes. Next came a girl with a rose in her hair, who rejected two different chairs before she finally and fussily dropped into the third.

"It's also *her* homeroom," a voice said, somewhere near her left ear. The puppy. He'd taken a seat next to her and was leaning so far over he was almost parallel to the floor.

"Huh?" she asked, simultaneously discovering that Sagittarians like to travel and checking out a swaggering guy in a T-shirt that seemed as though it had been through a shredder. He saw Deal looking at him and winked. She gave him a no-dice look.

"The ghost. This is where Al Benson saw her."

"Oh." Deal had scarcely heard him. Suddenly she sat up straighter in her seat, her attention caught by the latest arrivals. There were five of them, and they shone. Everyone was watching them. Even the heavy-metal boys looked their way and quickly pretended not to. It didn't take long for Deal to realize that their glow was reflected light. They were merely planets. The sun at their center was a very tall, very beautiful blond boy with a long-legged, equally beautiful blond girl by his side.

Six months, Deal guessed, studying the pair. They've been together six months. Maybe eight. He plays basketball. She's a cheerleader. They'll be king and queen of the Valentine's Day dance. Everyone thinks they're the perfect couple and they'll be together forever.

She felt a familiar tug somewhere in her solar plexus and a hot, dry murmur she'd heard too many times before in her head. *But you could change all that,* it said.

I could, but I don't want to, she countered.

She stared at the blond boy. Le Roi de Soleil, she thought, recalling one of the few phrases that had stuck with her from world history. The Sun King. Probably a Leo. She liked Leos. Jason was a Leo. Also Tommy and Claude and that other boy she'd dated, what was his name. He hadn't lasted long. Actually none of them had. The triumph was in the getting, not the keeping. Men are so gullible, Renee liked to say, but she was letting one lead her by the nose. Well, that wouldn't happen to her, Deal had decided years ago. "Love 'em and leave 'em" was her motto. Had *been* her motto. It and the Game were getting old.

This one's a real challenge, said the dry voice. *Maybe you can't handle him.*

Shut up, Deal snapped at it.

Then the Sun King looked at her.

For a moment, she just looked back. Then she gave him a small smile. She was not a stunner, and she knew it. She was a little too bony. Her chin was a bit short and she had a slight overbite. But she could, when she wanted to, make people believe that she was beautiful. She could make *him* think that. Right then and there.

Suddenly, she flinched, startled by a loud crash next to her.

The eager puppy was flat on the floor, his chair lying next to him.

Deal had the grace not to laugh.

"Oh, by the way. I'm Laurie Lorber," he said from his supine position. "Like the guy in *Little Women*. And in case you were wondering, I'm a Libra—sign of grace and beauty."

"I wasn't wondering," Deal replied wryly. Then she picked up her astrology book and read about the moon in Scorpio until the homeroom teacher walked in.

chapter two

The cafeteria was large, but not large enough. One look at it and Deal felt like a fox in a box. It hadn't been easy getting through the morning. She'd counted on lunchtime as a chance to escape. At her last school, the students had been allowed to go out to eat, giving them at least the illusion of freedom. But at Brain Rot, everyone had to stay in.

Surveying the scene, Deal recognized clumps of people from the classes she'd had so far. That kid Laurie "Sign of Grace and Beauty" Lorber wasn't one of them, which was funny because he'd been in all of her other classes. Thank God, she thought, with a small and peculiar twinge of . . . what? Disappointment? No way. She didn't want to sit with him. She didn't want to sit with anyone, really. But what did she want to do? She felt edgy. The rest of the term stretched before her, aimless, dreary.

But it doesn't have to be, said the dry voice. *Not if you were playing the Game.*

I told you to go away, she responded.

Straightening her back, she selected an empty table and sat in the single wan patch of sunlight that filtered through the grimy window. She had no food with her and didn't want any. Opening her astrology book, she stared at it without reading, her restlessness turning into dull detachment. She was wondering if she could spend the whole period that way, unmoving, alone, when the custodian, on his way to fix the ever-failing soda machine nearby, jostled her table with his toolbox. The book flipped out of her hands and onto the floor, landing at a girl's feet.

"What does it say about Leos?" the girl asked, picking up the book and holding it out to Deal. Her name was Tina. Tina Tchelichev (Deal had heard it mispronounced in two of the three classes they'd had together so far). She was the Sun King's girlfriend—the last person Deal expected to meet, the first she would have planned to if she'd been playing the Game—and she had a dab of jelly clinging to her cheek like a purple mole.

Deal eyed it with amusement, enjoying the temporary flaw on Tina's perfect face. Not nice, Deal, she told herself. And not necessary. She's not your rival. "You have some jelly on your cheek," she said, taking the book.

Tina wiped it away. "I'm such a sloppy eater," she said, so disingenuously that Deal, to her annoyance, found herself liking her. Then Tina turned to Jean Herrick, the elegant-looking, dark-skinned girl next to her.

"Why didn't *you* tell me I had food on my face?" she said, with mock irritation.

"I thought you'd let Mark lick it off," Jean replied.

"Cut it out," Tina complained nasally, blushing and swatting at her friend, who laughed. Deal's momentary warm feeling vanished. She deliberately returned to her book.

"So, what *does* it say about Leos?" Jean asked, trying to read it upside down.

Deal paused, wondering why she and Tina were continuing to be so friendly and curious enough to let them continue. "It says they're noble, dramatic, and natural leaders."

"Really?" said Tina. "That fits."

"You?"

"No. Mark." Tina, blushing again, nodded toward where the Sun King and his retinue sat.

Ha. I knew it. Deal suppressed a chuckle. She turned to look at him. He was looking back. Deal knew without being told that he'd been watching for a while. Tina waved. He saluted. Deal cut her eyes away from him.

"What else does it say?" Jean prodded. "Tell us the bad stuff."

"Well . . . Leos can be proud and vain," Deal said, which was true. "And faithless," she added, which wasn't.

"That fits, too." Jean laughed again. Deal thought she sounded like her former next-door neighbor's cockatoo.

14

Tina swatted her good-naturedly once more.

"Girl, you're just blind with love." Jean grinned at Deal, trying to make her an accomplice to the teasing.

Deal refused the role. "There isn't any other way to be in love, is there?" she said, raising an eyebrow.

"Ha," Jean snorted.

Out of the corner of her eye she caught a glimpse of Tina studying her with interest.

"You're new here, aren't you?" the blond girl asked.

"Yes," Deal replied noncommittally.

"You'll like it. It's a great school." The *only* great school, her tone implied. In her head Deal could hear Jean add, "As long as you're with the right crowd."

There was a slight pause, a moment of silent decision that passed between Jean and Tina. Deal waited for the verdict. When it came, she nearly laughed at the irony: "Why don't you sit with us?" Tina asked.

Deal didn't answer immediately. From where she was standing she could see Mark watching them again. She felt suddenly wide awake.

One final match, said the dry voice. *How can you resist?*

I can and I will. I'll tell them thanks, but no thanks. She glanced back at the girls. Jean's brow was furrowed. What are you waiting for? We're doing you a favor, her expression said. But Tina, to Deal's surprise, looked amused.

Deal closed her book. I *can* resist temptation, she

insisted silently. Watch me. "All right," Deal agreed at last.

"Good." Tina smiled and led her to their table. Jean walked a step behind her. It made Deal feel she was being examined.

"Do you believe that Walters? Read Act I of *Hamlet* by tomorrow," a thin, ruddy boy with high cheekbones and blond hair—though not as blond as the Sun King's—was complaining. "That's thirty-three pages. We're the only junior English class that has to read that play."

Carter Evans. Deal, practiced at remembering names, ticked off his on her mental list.

"That's because Walters is a Shakespeare wonk," said Mitch Jefferson, burly and beige and with the beginnings of a mustache. " 'To be or not to be . . .' " he recited in a quavering, overdramatic voice.

"To pee or not to pee," said Jean, and everyone laughed.

"What's the big deal about Shakespeare, anyway?" asked Carter, not quite willing to let the topic go.

"He left his wife his second-best bed in his will," Deal said.

Everyone looked at her, unsure how to respond, until Mark laughed. Then they all joined in, obviously thinking it was some kind of weird joke—which it wasn't, but rather one of the bits of strange trivia Deal liked to collect.

I bet that goofy kid Laurie would know that, Deal thought, wondering why she'd thought of something—someone—so irrelevant.

Tina touched Deal's hand. "Everybody, this is—" she began and stopped. "Who are you, anyway?" She giggled.

"Delia McCarthy," Deal said.

Tina nodded, like a teacher approving of a student's answer. "Delia McCarthy," she repeated.

"A newly, huh?" said Carter, pretending he wasn't looking at her chest while he looked at her chest.

"Yes," Deal replied, mimicking his eye movements.

"That's Carter," said Tina.

"At your service." He jumped up, clicked his heels, bowed, and sat back down.

Tina went around the table, making introductions. Deal didn't mention that she already knew most of their names. "And last, but not least . . ."

"Lust, but not beast," interjected Carter.

Tina rolled her eyes at him and continued, with a little flutter of pride in her voice, "This is Mark."

"Mark *Chelsom*," the Sun King said. He was leaning back languorously in his chair, but his eyes were sharp.

"Pleased to meet you," she said, giving him the same small smile she had in homeroom.

He smiled back. But his left pinkie tapped on the table. Deal looked pointedly at it and Mark stopped tapping. He looks guilty already—and I haven't even done anything, Deal thought. *Yet.* The word hovered ghostly and insinuating. Deal kicked it away.

"You'll like it here. It's a great school," Mark said, with the same inflection as Tina.

"I'm sure I will," said Deal, giving him another smile.

He began tapping his finger again.

Deal took a sip of soda. Mark turned to Tina. "Hey, did you bring me that Pepsi?" he demanded, somewhat brusquely.

Tina frowned. "Yes, my lord and master." She plunked it down in front of him.

"Whoa." "Pig." "Deck him," came the chorus of comments.

Mark reached out and put his arm around her. "Your lord and master humbly, double humbly, triple humbly thanks you. My lips thank you. My tongue thanks you. My throat thanks you. My stomach thanks you—"

"His dentist thanks you," Jean put in.

Tina, giggling, looked at Deal. "Should I forgive him?" she asked.

"I wouldn't," Deal said, deadpan. Everyone laughed. Only Deal knew she wasn't joking.

chapter three

───

Deal dropped her backpack next to the small hall table—the only place she was allowed to dump it, besides her room, according to Number 12 of Gram's Household Rules—and stared for a nanosecond at the postcard lying there. The picture of the soaring space-age arch on the front was a dead giveaway. Deal scooped up the card and flipped it over, reading as she walked to the kitchen:

Week 3, and St. Louis really is a great town. Clark's doing great—has the office running like clockwork already. I'm still looking for a job. Our new apartment is nice, but small. But there's always room for you on the couch. Come visit soon.

Love, Mom

"Right. Just don't stay very long," Deal muttered, already regretting the eagerness with which she'd read the note. What did she expect? That Renee would suddenly beg her to come live with her and that weasel-faced boyfriend of hers? Clark—would you believe Kent; his parents must be real comedians—had made it abundantly clear that he was "finished with raising children." That included his own, whom he was more than willing to abandon, along with his devoted wife, Deal thought contemptuously, knowing at the same time that she was exaggerating. Clark hadn't really been all that willing to leave his family, although he'd kept promising he would. For three years, Renee threatened to—and occasionally did—break off their relationship.

"He's such a liar," she'd say. "He'll never leave her." Then his devoted wife found out about him and Renee and kicked him out. Renee was ecstatic. There was just one catch. Clark was taking a job in another state. Renee was invited to move there with him—Deal was not. She put on a good show, Renee did. Sobbing for one whole day about how she could never desert her baby, then deciding to dump Deal with Gram the next.

Deal looked down at the card again. Instead of dots, her mother had, as usual, drawn hearts over all the "i" 's. Deal couldn't believe she'd ever found that cute. With a flick of her wrist, she shot the card across the room just as Gram entered it. The card landed at her feet.

Arching one brow, Gram picked it up and deposited it on the counter. Deal waited for the inevitable lecture on self-restraint or littering or whatever. But it didn't come. All Gram said was, "I got one, too."

"Yeah? What did yours say?" asked Deal. Her voice sounded like a fingernail that needed to be filed.

"Less than yours. Your mother's a woman of few words—except when she's talking."

Deal let out a snort. Then she said curiously, "How come you're not at work?"

"Ah. I wanted to offer you milk and cookies on your first afternoon home after your first day of school," Gram replied. She took a bag of Pepperidge Farm Milanos out of the cabinet, shook them onto a plate, and poured out a glass of milk. "Is that grandmotherly enough for you?" she said dryly.

"Yes, thanks," Deal replied, equally dryly. But she was moved by the unexpected kind gesture, no matter how coolly Gram tendered it. She leaned forward to hug her. Gram stiffly allowed herself to receive the embrace. A kiss would have been out of the question.

How could she have given birth to someone like Renee? Deal wondered, not for the first time. Deal's mother had a lot of faults, but coldness wasn't one of them. Renee was the touchy-feely type, always patting, holding, squeezing, nuzzling. On nights when Clark was unavailable and Deal didn't feel like going out, she and her mother would snuggle on the couch in front of the TV, falling all over themselves at a silly sitcom or burying their faces in each other's shoulders at some scary movie. Six months from now, Gram and I will still be sitting on opposite ends of the sofa—if we sit together at all, Deal thought.

Her anger returned. "Cheers," she said, lifting the glass in a bitter toast.

Gram moved to the counter and turned on the coffeemaker. "So, how was your day?" she asked. It sounded forced, as though she'd just studied a textbook on making conversation and this was her first practice session.

"Okay," Deal replied noncommittally.

"You get the subjects you wanted?"

"Yeah." Deal didn't think it necessary to tell Gram there were no subjects she wanted or, for that matter, didn't want.

"Delia, why do you settle for C's when you could be getting A's?" Mr. Mandel, the guidance counselor at her old high school, had once asked.

"I don't like angular letters," she'd answered.

"Flippant underacheiver," the counselor wrote.

" 'I' before 'e,' except after 'c,' " Deal, reading upside down, told him.

Mr. Mandel had soon let her go, with the request that she think about working harder. Deal said yes, she'd think about it, and startled the man by straightening his annoyingly crooked tie. On the way back to class she wondered what comment he'd make in her file about that.

"Did you meet any interesting people?" Gram persisted, drumming her fingers impatiently on the counter as she waited for her coffee to heat up.

"In high school?" Deal gibed.

Gram pursed her lips. It was obvious to Deal that she was annoyed, but not obvious why. She got that way often. Deal was not about to mention the Sun King or his circle. But in payment for the milk and cookies, she offered, "Well, there was one boy who was sort of amusing." She paused, surprised to find herself thinking about Laurie, and even more surprised to find herself smiling. "He told me something about the school having its own pet ghost—a woman in white."

"What nonsense!" Gram jeered. "I have no patience with superstitious people."

"Renee's superstitious," Deal said, through a mouthful of cookies, partly to needle Gram and partly because she couldn't help it—her mother kept creeping into her mind.

Anyway, it was true. Renee knocked on wood, avoided walking under ladders, carried a lucky stone, read her daily horoscope, and visited innumerable clairvoyants and fortune-tellers.

Once she took Deal with her to visit a psychic. The place they'd gone to was perfect—a large Victorian house with balconies and cupolas and plenty of wood and stone. A movie location scout couldn't have chosen a better set. But the psychic herself was another story. Tall and big-boned with a no-nonsense jaw, she looked as though she should be out planting trees instead of sitting indoors, telling people about the future. Deal remembered rather liking her until the woman fixed her with an intense stare and said, "This one will have dealings with the spirit world. She will have to finish the business someone else started." Then, spooked, Deal had dug her fingers into the chair's dark cat hair–covered velveteen cushion and fought the urge to run out of the room until Renee finally took her home.

"Oh, Renee," Gram dismissed, then warned, "I hope you don't intend to follow in her footsteps." Gram no doubt was referring to more than just her mother's superstitious leanings. "And don't talk with your mouth full," Gram finished.

Annoyed, Deal decided not to talk at all. The silence stretched between them like the long gray yarn she'd once unraveled from her mother's woolly sweater. Then Gram decided she'd had enough of it.

"I've got to get some groceries for dinner," she said, rising. She did not invite Deal to come along.

In less than two minutes, Gram was gone. Deal unhurriedly finished her milk and cookies, then rinsed out her glass and plate (Rule 6—"Do not leave dishes and silverware for me to wash"). Glancing around the neat kitchen, she noticed the phone book on its appointed shelf. Idly, she picked it up and flipped to the C's. Cheedham. Chelly. Chelsom, Carolyn. Chelsom, Mark Sr., 555-4454. Digging a line under the number with her nail, she recited it three times like a magic spell. "What am I doing?" she said aloud. Then shutting the book with a slap, she moved restlessly to the window.

A delivery boy on a bike was riding up to the house across the street, pedaling like he'd done this a hundred times before. But then he turned his head in Deal's direction, and whether he hit a bump, a stone, a twig in the road, or his foot twisted, or his hands slipped, his bike bucked and down he and it went. The box attached to the back popped open and two pizzas shot out of their cartons onto the road. The guy sat up, his cap dangling from one ear. It was Laurie. He saw her and grinned. She raised her hand in a half wave, then stopped herself. What *am* I doing? "Clown," she disposed of him, lowering her hand and ducking away from the window.

She looked around the kitchen. For a moment she felt stuck. Trapped, without an idea of how to fill up the next few minutes, let alone the rest of the afternoon. Then she wheeled around and strode purposefully toward Gram's bedroom, where, several days before, she'd begun systematically to go through her grandmother's closets and drawers. Deal wasn't sure what she was hoping to find there—some amusing memento, perhaps, some secret vice, some chink in Gram's formidable armor.

So far there'd been nothing all that amusing or indiscreet, just a few things that made Deal smile or wonder— a pink feather boa; a man's bow tie; a photo of Deal's grandfather, aged twenty-five or so, with Renee in his arms; a postcard, also from Granddad, from, of all places, St. Louis, where he'd gone on a business trip. "Miss you, miss you, miss you," it said. It was dated July 20, 1963. Gram had divorced him the following year.

Deal opened the closet and lifted down a hatbox. Gram was the only person she knew who still wore "fancy chapeaux," as Renee called them. The one in this box was blue with a round brim and a black band. Deal tried it on in front of the mirror. "Yuck," she said. Behind the hatbox was another hatbox, which Deal also took down. She opened it and nearly shrieked, thinking there was a dead bird inside. But it was a ridiculous cloche covered with pheasant feathers. Deal didn't even want to try that one on. Standing on the small step stool Gram kept in the closet, Deal was about to replace the hat when she noticed a small metal file box wedged in the back of the shelf. She lifted it down and tried to open it, but it was locked.

Maybe her will is inside, she thought. But she couldn't imagine Gram hiding her will in the closet. And this box was definitely hiding. Grabbing a pin off the dresser, she tried to pick the lock. But the pin bent. I need something stronger, she thought. Tweezers, maybe. Deal was about to open the drawer where they were kept when she heard the sound of a car pulling into the driveway.

Quickly, she shoved the metal box and the two hatboxes back on the shelf and the step stool into the closet, shut both closet and bedroom door, and was sitting in the kitchen when Gram entered, frowning.

"That was a fast trip," Deal said, trying not to pant.

"Forgot my money. Stupid of me," Gram said gruffly. Deal knew she disliked making a mistake, loathed even more admitting it. Gram took a few bills from a teapot on the counter and stomped out.

Deal took a deep breath and released it. "Whew," she said.

Out in the hallway, she glanced in the direction of Gram's room. "Uh-uh." She shook her head. "Don't tempt fate. It'll keep." Then she went into the living room and turned on the TV.

chapter four

"Shakespeare was a writer who knew how to grab his audience," Mr. Walters, pink with excitement over his favorite author, boomed. "Wouldn't you agree, Mr. Chelsom?"

How to Teach High School, Lesson One: Get the class leader on your side. Deal nearly snickered. Teachers were so transparent.

"Absolutely, Mr. Walters," Mark replied smoothly, without a trace of mockery, while under his desk his hands rhythmically squeezed and released a grip strengthener.

"Look at the first line of *Hamlet*: 'Who's there?' " Mr. Walters continued. "That starts the play with a bang."

Jean's books fell on the floor next to Deal's desk with a bang of their own. The class laughed. Jean reached down to pick them up and slipped Deal a note. She opened it behind her book. "I'm baby-sitting after school today. Want to come over? Tina," it said.

For the second time in the space of a few minutes Deal wanted to laugh. She'd be seeing Tina next period at lunch, so there was no need for her to send a note. But sending notes in class was so full of safe little intrigue, so *high school,* that it figured Tina would do it. It was probably the most daring thing she ever did.

Deal couldn't see Tina from where she was sitting without twisting in her seat, which she was not about to do, but out of the corner of her eye she noticed Jean, the ever-faithful lady-in-waiting, giving Deal a hurry-up-and-answer signal with her expressive eyebrows. What a pair they were, expecting her to be so flattered to join their little clique. Well, a part of her was flattered. Just a tiny part, but it irritated her.

Deal looked at the note again, scanning it for other information. So, she realized, Tina wasn't going extracurricular today, and Mark was. He'd be on the basketball court, looking blond and sweaty and cute in gym shorts. Well, so what? The information was useless. Even if she wanted to, which she didn't, she wasn't going to be there to see him. She wasn't the extracurricular type. Not really. Except for . . .

She picked up a pen. "Can't," she scrawled on Tina's note. "Glee club." She folded up the paper, but didn't deliver it. Squeezing and unsqueezing it in her lap, in a conscious imitation of the Sun King, she turned back to Mr. Walters.

". . . and just a few lines later, Shakespeare lets us

know why these men are so agitated," he was saying. "Marcellus says, 'What, has this thing appeared again tonight?' "

"My thing appears every night," Carter interrupted.

Mark, departing from his regal manner, high-fived him across the aisle. Everyone else giggled, except Deal, who never found that kind of humor funny, and Laurie, sitting to her right, who was actually reading the play.

"I'd suggest a cold shower, Mr. Evans," said Mr. Walters, and everyone laughed again. "Now, what is Marcellus referring to?"

Laurie raised his hand.

"Mr. Lorber?" the teacher called on him.

"A ghost. Hamlet, Senior, to be precise," he answered. He glanced at Deal, his face shining with schoolboy enthusiasm.

It figures. A nerd as well as a klutz, Deal thought. But there was something charming, maybe even admirable, about his undisguised delight, and she couldn't help smiling.

"Correct," Mr. Walters roared so forcefully that his jowls shook. "A ghost. As like Hamlet's father, the late king, 'as thou art to thyself.' Now, in Shakespeare's day, most people believed in ghosts. But they didn't all believe the same things about them. Some people thought that a ghost was bad news—an evil spirit that always foretold disaster. Others felt that a ghost was an uneasy spirit, one that had some unfinished business to settle. What do you people think about ghosts? Do they exist?"

"Yes," yelled out part of the class. "No," called out another. "Maybe," rang out Laurie's voice.

"Maybe?" asked Mr. Walters.

"I'd like to believe in them," Laurie explained. "If ghosts are possible, anything is."

"Yeah, anything—like zombies, demons, aliens from space . . . Then the world would be totally out of control," said Carter.

Privately, Deal agreed with him. But she didn't care to admit it.

"Well, I believe in ghosts," Tina announced without even waiting for Mr. Walters to call on her. "My grandmother saw one in Russia. It was a white blob, sort of like a giant snowball—and just as cold." She looked at Mark. So did the rest of the class.

"I believe in basketball," he replied.

"Me, too," said Carter. "Also burgers and babes."

"What about the Brain Rot ghost?" asked Tina. "Don't you believe in her?"

"Yeah," Jean backed her up. "People say she's the ghost of a girl who was hit by a car near here forty years ago."

"No," said another girl. "She was a kid who killed herself forty years ago when she got left back."

"You're both wrong," said Carter. "She's the ghost of a teacher who went crazy forty years ago from reading too much Shakespeare."

Everyone laughed, even Mr. Walters.

Deal laughed with them, mechanically. Then she glanced down at the cover of her book—a corny picture of Hamlet Jr. shrinking back from the ghost of his papa—and her mind shifted suddenly to her own father. He'd flitted in and out of her life like a ghost, leaving her with two strong memories: a constant smell of tobacco and the click of the "lucky dice" he always carried. "Watch out. Snake eyes," he'd say. When he left that was what Renee called him. "That creep Snake Eyes." Gone now and pretty much forgotten, except when Deal caught a whiff of Camels or saw a guy rolling dice.

"We haven't heard from our new student. Ms. McCarthy?"

Deal blinked at the teacher. He repeated her name, and an answer tumbled out of her mouth. "I don't believe in fathers," she said.

There was a pause before the class erupted. Deal could feel waves of approval washing over her, everyone appreciating her cleverness, her irreverence. Normally, she was used to that. But now she felt oddly disconcerted, a feeling amplified by the curious look she was getting from Laurie.

"Well, Ms. McCarthy, perhaps if Hamlet felt that way, too, he'd have been alive at the end of the play. . . ." He turned to the board then. The timing could not have been better. Deal, regaining the poise no one knew she'd lost, rose swiftly and pitched Tina's note. It sailed clear over Jean's desk and landed neatly on the one next to it—Mark's.

Strike one, said the dry voice.

I didn't mean to do that, she protested, looking at Jean.

The girl rolled her eyes. Later, she and Tina would tease Deal about her wretched aim. And Deal would let them. The truth was she had a good arm.

Deal made an "oops" face and Jean gesticulated frantically until Mr. Walters turned around again. He never saw them, nor did he catch Mark, who, with lazy amusement, opened and read the note, then glanced, not at Tina, but at Deal.

However, Deal caught it, clear across the room. Watch out, she thought, not knowing whether she was talking to Mark or to herself. Snake Eyes.

chapter five

"Hot dog, that Hamlet was one Great Dane," Laurie said, loping alongside Deal in the corridor, sticking with her like a horsefly on a pony. Their last class of the day was over, and Deal was on her way to glee club, a fact that struck her as somewhat absurd.

"Spare me," she told Laurie. English had been hours ago. She couldn't believe this goofball had saved up that silly joke all this time. Then again, she thought, with a quick glance at his gap-toothed grin, yes, she could.

"That was a good class, don't you think? Especially all that stuff about ghosts," Laurie said.

"Not really," Deal rebuffed, slipping through two arguing seniors.

Laurie tried to follow, bumped one of the debaters, and dropped his books.

Deal didn't stop to help him. She pushed ahead quickly, but a teacher with an armful of posters, followed by a quartet of freshmen, walking so close they looked like the first-ever set of Siamese quadruplets, slowed her down and gave Laurie time to catch up.

"That's a nice house you live in," he said, trying a different tack. "Your parents have good taste."

"It's my grandmother's house," Deal told him.

"Oh. Then *she* has good taste. Does she still live there?"

"Where else would she live?"

"Oh. Yeah. Well, I guess it's big enough for all of you."

"All of who?"

"You and your parents and your grandma."

"My parents don't live there," Deal replied coolly.

"Oh," Laurie said, abashed. *"Oh,"* he repeated, as if something suddenly made sense to him. He stopped talking. Deal waited for him to put his other foot in his mouth, but instead he finally said quietly, "That must be hard. My folks can be royal butt-aches, but I wouldn't not want them around."

It was the same gentle, concerned tone he'd used at their first meeting when he'd asked her if she missed her friends. This time it got to her. She turned and looked, really looked at him, taking in his soft eyes, large as a German shepherd's, the peach fuzz on his cheeks, the freckles over his nose, and she suddenly, astonishingly, imagined herself laying her head on his shoulder while he stroked her hair.

She twitched her shoulders to get rid of the image. "Lucky for you. Who else would put up with your blabbering?" she thrust.

He recoiled, his eyes filled with stunned hurt. Deal was immediately rueful. Striking at him was as cruel as smacking a puppy with a rolled-up newspaper. "Sorry," she muttered. "I'm sure your folks are nice."

Laurie had amazing recuperative powers. "Maybe you'd like to meet them sometime," he suggested hopefully, practically wagging his tail.

Deal shook her head. "Thanks, but I don't think so," she said, not unkindly. Now, shoo, go on home, she felt like adding as she reached the music room.

But Laurie didn't leave. Instead, he grinned. "Well, howzaboutdat? A room with a déjà vu!"

"What?"

"You, me, glee club," he said, grunting like Tarzan, pointing at each thing he named. Then, in his normal voice, he added, "Dumb name, glee club. Sounds like a bunch of laughing devils chasing people with pitchforks."

Deal was tickled. "I've always thought it sounded like Santa and his elves ho-hoing away at the North Pole. I think I like your idea better." She smiled at him—a genuine smile.

He smiled back. Then he opened the door and they both went inside.

Laurie took a seat with the other tenors. Deal signed the attendance sheet and looked around the room.

Mr. Ferrara, the choral director, who was also Deal and Laurie's homeroom teacher, stepped in front of her. Everything about him was precise and tailored—his beard, his suit, his words. "May I help you?" he asked.

"Is that the soprano section?" she asked, nodding at the larger of the two groups of seated girls. Ms. Baines, Deal's eighth-grade music teacher, had told her she was a soprano, and a good one. She urged Deal to join a church choir. "You could be a soloist," Ms. Baines said. But church choir was not as interesting as Jimmy Cohen, whom Deal was dating at the time, so she nixed the idea.

"Yes. Why?" Mr. Ferrara replied.

"Because I'm a soprano," Deal said, as deliberately as if she were talking to an alien.

"Ah. You wish to join our group?" Mr. Ferrara said.

No, I'm just doing a survey on annoying teachers. "Yes," Deal said carefully. She could feel everyone staring. She heard buzzing and giggling.

"Fine. Then you have to audition."

"What?" Deal laughed in disbelief.

"You have to audition," the director repeated, switching roles so that now Deal was the visitor from outer space.

"You didn't have to audition for chorus at my last

school," Deal said—at least that's what Tom, the one with the big hands and bigger voice, had told her.

"This is not a chorus, my dear. It's a glee club." My glee club, his snooty voice implied, gleefully. "To join it, I require an audition."

You know what you can do with your audition, Deal wanted to say, and leave. But she couldn't back down now. Pride wouldn't let her. "All right," she said.

"Then come," said Mr. Ferrara, beckoning her to the piano. "Can you sight-sing?" he asked, thrusting a piece of music at her.

"No," said Deal.

"Pity," Mr. Ferrara said, with none in his voice.

"Can't I just sing something I know?" Deal said.

"Like what? 'Happy Birthday to You'?" the director sniffed. The glee club tittered. "For my audition, you sing what I want you to sing."

Deal felt her anger rise. *His* glee club. *His* audition. *His* rules. He'd be a perfect mate for Gram. She stared stonily at him.

When he realized that she was not about to budge, he said, "All right. I'll play the soprano part twice. Let's see how quickly you can learn it."

Deal looked down at the words as he played—some nonsense about springtime, the pretty ring time. The melody was not difficult. And Deal had a knack for picking up tunes as soon as she heard them. A rare talent, Ms. Baines had said. So, by the time Mr. Ferrara said, "Now you try it," she knew it by heart.

She sang it full and clear. When she finished, there was a momentary silence. Then Laurie began to applaud. The fool, Deal thought, without acknowledging him. Mr. Ferrara looked at her with approval. "Very nice," he said. "Very, very nice . . ." He consulted the sign-up sheet briefly—too briefly. "Delilah."

"Delia," Laurie corrected.

The rest of the glee club nudged one another and tittered again.

Deal paid no attention to them. "Did I pass?" she said coldly.

The teacher gave a little laugh. "Yes. You passed."

"Where do I sit?"

"Front row, seat two. Soprano section."

Deal nodded curtly and took her seat. She continued to ignore everyone around her, including, or especially, Laurie, while the sopranos, the altos, and the baritones all learned their parts in the springtime/ring-time madrigal. Then it was the tenors' turn.

"Laurie, will you demonstrate the tenor part, please?" asked Mr. Ferrara.

"Sure," he replied, while Deal sat, dog-earing the page. But when he opened his mouth, her head jerked up and around. He sang—there was no way to describe it other than a cliché—like an angel. He made Deal feel that the world was full of undiscovered glory—and, even more unexpectedly, that she was.

You can't be serious. You can't find that one attractive, the dry voice whispered in her head.

Of course not, she told it. She turned away from Laurie, refusing to look at him again for the rest of the rehearsal. When it ended, she bounded swiftly out the door into the hallway, where the Sun King and his courtier, Carter, stood examining a trophy case. Their timing could not have been more perfect—and she wondered if that was intentional.

They turned slowly when she approached.

"Hi, Delia," said Carter.

"Hi," she answered, looking at Mark. She felt the rush of an old, welcoming excitement. It would be so easy to accept it. So easy.

"So, you like to sing," he said, as if the idea amused him.

"It passes the time." She shrugged, more calmly than she felt.

There was a pause. Then Mark said, "We just had basketball practice."

No kidding, Deal thought. "Are you good?" she asked. "Are you a good player?"

"Yeah," he answered. No false modesty there. "Carter's good, too," he added.

"Truer words were never spoken," said Carter. He and Mark high-fived.

Look at them. They can toss a ball into a basket and they think they own the world. "That's good to know," Deal responded. "I hate being lied to."

"Yeah? I'll bet." Mark's voice was cool, but his eyes held a challenge.

It's time to take him up on it, murmured the dry voice.

"I've gotta go," she said to Mark and Carter, and began to walk away.

"Need a ride home?" Carter called.

Deal hesitated. "Where's your car?"

"In my dreams. But Mark's is in the parking lot."

The rest of the glee club had been steadily filing out of the music room. From the corner of her eye, Deal saw Laurie emerge. He looked at her, puzzled.

Go ahead. Take a ride. You know you want to, the voice whispered, more urgently.

Leave me alone, she told it. Go away! I don't need this. I don't want this! "No, thanks. I need the fresh air," she told Mark and Carter and hurried out of the school.

Out on the street she breathed in chill air, scarcely noticing how it stung her throat. Her face was warm, her mind confused. She needed to clear it.

You're losing your grip, said the voice.

I'm losing nothing. I never lose.

You'll never win—if you don't play the Game.

I told you—I don't want to play the Game anymore.

What do you want? That puppy? Or maybe you'd prefer nothing, no one at all.

"Deal!" Mark's voice made her turn her head sharply. His car, an old blue BMW, lovingly polished, moved slowly along the curb. "Come on. Get in."

She paused, torn. It would be so easy to give in. So easy and so painless. And after all, the Game *was* exhilarating, wasn't it? It made her feel so powerful, so alive. Without it, what was she? What would she do day after drab day? Who would she be?

Your move, said the voice.

"Yeah, Deal," Carter yelled over Mark's shoulder. "We don't bite."

She looked at them both, so cavalier, so cocky, and let out her breath. She smiled, brushing back her hair. "But I do," she said, and got into the car.

chapter six

The rules were always the same, the strategies always different. That was what made the Game such fun. And fun was what Deal was having. Why had she even tried to resist playing? she wondered as she slid into the front seat of Mark's car after he dropped off Carter.

The Sun King took his time making conversation, and Deal let him. He flicked on the radio. Deal expected to hear hard rock blare out and was surprised when violins sobbed from the speakers.

"So, you're a big-city girl, huh?" he said at last.

"I wouldn't exactly call Redland a big city," she replied.

"That's because you're not from Parkington." He nodded at the windshield to indicate their surroundings.

"Parkington doesn't seem like such a bad place."

"Not bad—just ordinary."

"Not so ordinary. You've got your resident ghost," Deal said lightly.

Mark snorted. "I don't believe in ghosts."

"So I noticed," Deal said to his handsome profile.

He grinned and took a left turn a little too fast. The tires squealed.

Ooh, you're so bad, Deal wanted to laugh at him. She settled back in her seat. "Have you ever been to Redland?" she asked.

"Yeah, a few times. To some games at the college."

"You planning on going there?"

"Tina is," Mark said, his tone distancing himself from his girlfriend.

Deal filed that information under "Useful." "You don't want to?" she asked.

"Hell, no!" Mark exclaimed. "I want to go to Georgetown or Duke."

Basketball schools. It figures, she thought.

But then he surprised her. "But I'll probably end up at Redland," he said.

"Because of Tina?" Deal suggested.

Mark shook his head. "Because I'm from Parkington, and that's where everyone from Parkington ends up." There was no bitterness in his voice, just an almost wistful resignation.

"Even you?" Deal said incredulously.

He smiled crookedly. "Yeah. Even me."

Deal didn't return the smile. She didn't like him like

this—vulnerable, yielding, and human—a mere mortal instead of a king. She didn't like that he'd revealed that part of himself to her, either. It made her uncomfortable. It was too intimate—or, rather, intimate in a way she hadn't reckoned on. It didn't follow the rules of the Game.

Mark thought better of it himself. Gunning the car through a yellow light, he said, "Anyway, Redland's not a bad town, right? Bet you miss your boyfriend there."

"Yeah. All of them." This time Deal did toss him a smile.

He snickered, glanced in the rearview mirror and smoothed back a lock of his golden hair. "Sounds like Redland guys weren't so hot if you went through so many of them."

"They were hot enough," said Deal.

The car was stopped at a red light. Mark looked at her a little too long. The car behind them honked. "Blow it out your ear," he yelled and peeled away.

"Enjoying the music?" he said, slowing down a little a few minutes later.

"Not really," she said. "I don't like classical."

"Neither do I," he said with a laugh, and punched up some hard rock.

Deal smiled to herself, pleased again with him, with herself, with the Game.

A moment later, she said, "This is it," and Mark rolled into her driveway.

"See you around," he said.

"Yeah, around," she agreed and got out of the car. She walked into the house without turning to wave good-bye.

It was only after he drove away that she realized she'd left her pack at school.

Damn, she thought. She needed that pack. It had her bus pass, her money, her books, her homework assignments in it. She'd have to go back and get it—and she'd have to walk.

Earlier she would have welcomed it. But now a light snow was falling, and it was already getting dark. Deal shivered, as much over the time of day as the cold. As far back as she could remember, she'd always disliked twilight. That in-between time where nothing seemed certain unnerved her.

She'd once told her mother about her fear, but Renee hadn't understood. "I don't know why you don't like sundown. To me it's a cozy time. A time to head home and settle down for the night," Renee had said.

"Is that what you're doing now, Mom? Settling down in your small apartment with Mr. Clark Kent, who for sure is no Superman?" muttered Deal, suddenly angry at her mother, at Clark, at her own stupidity and forgetfulness, which was making her take this hike.

A woman passing by gave her a look.

Deal made a geek face at her, and the woman scurried past up the path to her house.

Her earlier good mood totally dissipated, Deal trudged on, part of her wishing someone would stop and offer her a ride and a cup of coffee, the other part wanting to be invisible. When she finally reached Brain Rot, the snow was falling more thickly and the light was almost gone. The school was dark and silent. A perfect time to meet the Lady in White. "Right, Laurie?" she mocked out loud. But at that moment she wouldn't have minded if he'd been there to answer her. She jogged to the front door. It was locked.

She tried the back entrance next. It was locked, too.

"Damn!" she swore again, this time out loud.

She walked around to the other side of the building, where 513, the music room, was. The shades were drawn, but she could see a light behind them. "All right!" she breathed, relieved. Someone was still there. One window was partly open. It had been stuck that way for weeks. Mr. Benson hadn't gotten around to repairing it yet. Through it she could hear the piano, muffled and hesitant, as though someone was trying to pick out a melody.

Deal raised her hand to rap on the glass. But then she wavered. The would-be piano player was weeping. For a moment Deal weighed courtesy versus need. Need won. She knocked on the window. The piano plunking and the crying grew louder. She knocked again, and they were louder still. Concerned now, she tried to open the other windows. They were all locked. Cursing loudly, she jerked roughly at the one that was stuck, and suddenly it slid up as smoothly as if it had been oiled.

The piano was crashing and discordant now; the weeping had changed to wailing. The sounds rattled Deal's teeth, rippled icily over her skin. She hesitated again, then bravely hoisted herself up onto the sill, raised the shade, and jumped into the room. She got just a hazy glimpse of the figure at the piano—a slight figure all in white bathed in a misty glow—before it vanished, plunging the room into darkness.

"Hey!" she yelled. "Turn on the lights! Somebody turn on the lights!" She fumbled through the room, arms outstretched, looking for the switch. "Turn them on!" she bellowed again, cracking her knee against a chair.

Her fingers found the switch at last just as the hall lights flicked on and someone came through the door. She bumped into him and shrieked.

"Who are you? What are you doing here?"

"I might ask the same of you," said the short, very short, balding man. "I'm Mr. Benson, the custodial engineer." He looked keenly at her.

"I'm Deal . . . Delia Mc-McCarthy," she stammered. She forced herself to take a deep breath. "I left my pack here. I tried the doors, but they were locked," she explained carefully.

"Why didn't you ring the bell?"

"What bell?"

"The one at the front door. If you'd rung it, I would have let you in."

"Oh. I'm sorry. I didn't know there was a bell."

"Well, now you do. Remember it for next time."

"There won't be a next time," Deal said curtly. Trying not to shake, she went and got her pack. It was where she'd left it—under her seat.

"I'll let you out the back door," Mr. Benson said. "It's closer."

They walked down the corridor. Neither said a word until they got to the door.

Then pointedly he said, "You saw her, didn't you?"

"Who?" said Deal.

"The ghost. You saw her." His eyes were sharp, searching her face.

Deal stared back, willing herself not to blink. "I saw nothing," she said. "Nothing."

The custodian stared at her. It was clear he didn't know whether or not to believe her. Finally, he opened the door.

"Thank you," she said, stepping outside. The cold wind blew snow into her face.

"If you want, I can drive you home," Mr. Benson offered.

"Oh, no. I'm not far. I'll walk," she replied, setting off at a clip.

All the way home she barely felt the snow and the cold. She was too busy telling herself, It wasn't real. I know it wasn't. But then what was it? By the time she reached Gram's she'd convinced herself that she'd just been the victim of a nasty joke, and she swore vengeance on whoever had played it.

chapter seven

▬▬▬▬▬▬

She was thinking about her old bathrobe. The cuffs were frayed, the moss green had faded to the color of an unwatered lawn, and there was that orange juice stain shaped like the state of Illinois down the front. The robe had originally belonged to Renee—the last Christmas gift Deal's dad had given her. Renee had tried to throw it away when he left, but Deal had fished it out of the garbage and slept wrapped in it for a week until Renee finally agreed to let her keep it.

But Renee had never stopped hating it. On the day Deal was packing, her mother had handed her a new, pristine white robe. "Here's something a little nicer for Gram's," she'd said.

Deal had shoved it in the suitcase along with the old robe. But when she'd unpacked at Gram's, the old robe was gone. Renee must have plucked it out and thrown it away when Deal wasn't looking. To Deal, it was the crowning insult on top of the supreme betrayal.

Still, Deal wished she could see Renee now, wished she were back in that old familiar bathrobe, in their old apartment, in her hometown where there were no ghosts. Scratch that, fool. There are no ghosts here, either. Just practical jokers. Remember that . . .

"Aren't you feeling well?" Gram interrupted her thoughts. She looked pointedly at Deal's plate, still piled with most of her dinner. Deal blinked. "I'm fine," she said brusquely, taking a bite of veal cutlet. The breading was too thick and the piece turned to glue in her mouth. She forced herself to swallow it. It *had* to be a practical joke, she thought. Someone using a projector . . . or maybe mirrors. Aren't those things always done with mirrors?

The phone rang and Deal jumped. Gram gave her a curious look. When Deal didn't make a move to pick it up, Gram rose crisply and answered it.

"Hello . . . Yes, she is. May I ask who's calling?" She held the receiver against her chest. "It's someone named Tina," she said. "I'm glad you're making friends, but could you tell them not to call at dinnertime? I don't like having my meal interrupted."

"Such as it is," Deal muttered. Gram's cooking struck her as eminently interruptable.

"What did you say?"

Without replying, Deal held out her hand for the phone.

"Hi. How was glee club?" Tina asked after Deal's greeting.

Glee club? Why was she asking about that? Deal wondered suspiciously. "Okay," she replied flatly. "How was baby-sitting?"

"I'm still doing it. It's . . . hold it . . . Katie, honey, don't put that in your mouth. Throw it away . . . No, throw it *away!*"

Deal shut her eyes, as if that might block out Tina's struggles with her charge, and thought about the ghost prank. Who could have done it—or would have wanted to? Obviously, Tina was too otherwise engaged for practical jokes. Tina's friend Jean? She seemed like the type. Carter, too—but would he have made it back to school so fast? And how would he or Jean or anybody know she'd be going back there?

You're being paranoid, Deal, she told herself. Paranoid and dumb. You probably weren't the intended victim. Maybe the prankster was trying to get that janitor's goat. He seemed to believe in the ghost. Lots of people probably knew that, and in a hick town like Parkington, some of them would probably think it the thrill of a lifetime to give him a good scare.

". . . So, do you want to?" Tina said.

"Sure," Deal said. That's got to be it, she finished silently.

"Great," said Tina. "Saturday, then . . . Katie, leave it alone . . ."

Deal opened her eyes. She had no idea what Tina was rattling on about, hadn't even realized she'd answered her.

A crash and the sound of a kid crying filled the phone. "Katie! Gotta go. Tomorrow," Tina babbled and hung up.

Deal replaced the receiver and the phone immediately rang again.

"Hello," Deal answered.

"Is Maureen there?" a deep male voice inquired. A sixth sense told Deal the call was not about work.

"May I ask who's calling?

"Just a moment," she said, after he'd told her, and held the receiver against her chest, just as Gram had done. "It's someone named Winston. Shall I tell him he shouldn't call during dinner?"

Gram pursed her lips, but there was a flicker of amusement in her eyes. Touché, it said. She took the phone and moved out into the hallway. She could've taken the call in her room, but Deal knew that then Gram would be admitting that the call was special, and that wasn't her style.

Straining to listen, Deal heard nothing but muffled yeses and noes. She went back to the table, sliced off three-quarters of her cutlet, and dumped it, along with two-thirds of the mashed potatoes and string beans, into the garbage. She was sitting down, toying with the remainder of the food, when Gram returned.

Silently, Gram sat down and began to eat the rest of her dinner. Surreptitiously, Deal studied her. Gram's face was impassive, but there were faint streaks of pink across her high cheekbones.

It was several minutes before Deal said, "He has a nice voice."

A string bean slid off Gram's fork. She speared and ate it slowly. Then she patted her lips. "I may be going out Friday night," she said casually.

When Deal didn't reply, Gram, perhaps feeling that that was a bit begrudging, even for her, added, "Ice skating."

"Dress warmly," Deal said.

Gram's lips twitched in a smile. She got up to wash the dishes.

Deal dried, without having to be asked. Then she and Gram went into the living room to watch *Wheel of Fortune*, to which they were both—somewhat surprisingly—addicted. Instead of sitting at her end of the couch, Deal moved a foot toward the middle. Gram did the same.

"Dinner at Eight!" They both sang out the answer seconds before the contestant did. They looked at each other and laughed. Deal found herself beginning to relax.

Then a commercial came on for the movie *Ghost*, which was going to be shown on TV later that evening, and her tension returned.

"They were talking about the school ghost today in English," she said, trying to sound nonchalant, bits and pieces of the discussion floating into her mind. She waited for Gram to sneer at her again for mentioning something superstitious.

But instead, Gram, with a slight laugh, said, "Oh?

That's what you're learning in class? Perhaps I ought to complain to the board."

"We're reading *Hamlet*," Deal said, by way of explanation.

"Ah." Gram understood.

Deal paused. Then she continued carefully, "Everybody seemed to have heard a different story about who the ghost was. . . ." Then something struck her. "The only thing they agreed on was that she died about forty years ago. . . . Weren't you going to Blain Schott then?"

"Yes," Gram said, blandly.

"Do you know how this ghost rumor got started?" Deal asked, trying not to appear too curious.

"No. I don't," Gram replied coolly. She stood up and flicked off the TV. "Well, I'm sure you've got homework to do. Act II of *Hamlet*, perhaps?" She stood there until Deal had no choice but to get up and go to her room.

She lay on her bed, looking at the ceiling. There was a plaster rosette in the center. If she squinted, she could make out a spectral face among the curlicues.

"Whooo!" she moaned softly. "Whoooo! I'm gonna haunt you, Gram." She shivered. Then she began to laugh. Ridiculous. It's all ridiculous. A practical joke. An *impractical* joke. There are no such things as ghosts. None. Got that, Delia McCarthy? She slapped her cheeks and picked up *Hamlet*.

She fell asleep reading the play and dreamed about dancing on a piano with Laurie. The two of them were laughing, having a good time. Then the ghost came in. "Release me!" she quavered. "Release me!" Deal woke with a start, sweating. Her room was bright. She hadn't turned off the lights, hadn't even gotten ready for bed.

Slowly, shakily, she undressed and slipped into her nightshirt. She wondered if Laurie was asleep and if he was dreaming of her. What difference does that make, she told herself. But she found it comforting nonetheless. She held on to the idea like a stuffed teddy bear and settled back down under the covers, humming the spring-time/ring-time song until she finally fell back to sleep.

chapter eight

There had to be some glue on the floor. That was the only way to explain why Deal's feet were stuck outside of Room 513.

It was nine o'clock in the morning, the room was full of people, and wailing women in white were nowhere to be seen. There was nothing to be afraid of—if Deal was afraid, which, she told herself, she wasn't. Who could be afraid of a practical joke?

"Hey, you're not by any chance waiting for me?" Laurie said, appearing beside her.

Not by any chance, Deal would've said. But her mouth was moving as slowly as her feet, and all that came out of it was "Laurie!" uttered with an all-too-evident sigh of relief.

He squinted at her. "Are you okay?"

"Of course I am," she protested, but couldn't resist adding, "Why?"

"You look like . . . I don't know . . . like I woke you from a dream, and it was a weird one."

"All of my dreams are weird," Deal tossed. "Aren't yours?"

"Not all of them," he said and blushed. For once he seemed grateful when the bell rang.

His discomfort released her. Suddenly she had no trouble at all moving. Smiling, she sashayed into homeroom.

The steady, soothing background buzz of people patter was noticeably missing. Instead there was just Tina's voice—not loud, but edgy enough to have attracted everyone's attention.

"Because they're dangerous, that's why," she was saying as she waved a magazine in the air.

"Not in the right hands," Mark responded with some heat.

"Ha!"

"And they're less polluting than cars," he continued.

"As if you care about pollution," Tina shot back.

There were scattered titters in the room.

Mark glowered at the sources. Then he noticed Deal. "Hey," he said

"Hey," she replied, keeping her face carefully neutral. *A fight,* said the dry voice in her head. Yeah, and I'm not even the cause of it, she added.

"And besides, what about *noise* pollution?" Tina,

refusing to let go of the argument, waved the magazine again.

Carter plucked it out of her hand. "Catch!" he called, tossing it to Deal, who caught it neatly. The title jumped out at her in flashy orange letters: *Motorcycle Madness.*

"Carter!" Tina yelled, outraged.

"Get rid of the evidence," Carter went on.

"Should I bury it or burn it?" Deal asked dryly, but Carter's answer got lost in Mr. Ferrara's entrance. "Damn all copy machines!" he roared, wiping at a smudge of toner on his cream-colored shirt. Since Mr. Ferrara— unlike Mr. Walters—was not given to roaring, the effect was startling.

"Yeah, you tell 'em!" Carter hollered. From around the room came assorted whistles and cheers.

Shoving the magazine into her notebook, Deal crossed the room and dropped into her seat next to Laurie.

"Here. Hand these out." Mr. Ferrara plopped a bunch of notices on Carter's desk, then proceeded to blare out the attendance like an overactive trumpet. "Is that everybody? Good," he growled. Picking up a music score, he retreated behind it momentarily, looked up and announced, "Laurie and Delia, please stay after homeroom," then retreated again.

What is this? Deal's eyebrows said to Laurie.

He shrugged, but she detected a shifty little twinkle in his eyes that said if he wasn't absolutely sure, he could make a good guess.

Annoyed, she turned toward the Sun King. He and Tina were avoiding each other's eyes. *Opportunity knocks,* said the dry voice. It does indeed, Deal replied, opening her book and looking down at the magazine hidden there. One page was dog-eared. It revealed a picture of a large black-and-silver Harley. Deal studied it like a poker player assessing her hand. Then she tucked the magazine neatly back into her notebook where it would stay clean and safe and oh so useful for her next call.

She felt magnanimous enough to read a few pages of *Hamlet* before homeroom ended. Maybe I'll even raise my hand today and give Walters a thrill, she thought. Then she slowly made her way to Mr. Ferrara's desk.

Laurie, with obvious eagerness, was already there.

Mr. Ferrara looked up at them. "You don't have to purse your lips that way, Delia. I can promise you I'm not about to propose anything distasteful."

You don't know what I'd find distasteful, Deal, unaware that she'd been doing any pursing, thought. "I'm glad to hear that, Mr. Ferrara," she said.

"I'd like you both to listen to something. . . . Don't worry about your next class; I'll give you a pass." Moving from his desk to the piano, the teacher sat down, set out a piece of music, and began to play. The song was lyrical, romantic, and old—not Ludwig van Beethoven old, but more like great-grandmother time. It reminded Deal of a silvery-white gown—out of fashion, but still stunning, worn in the moonlight by a radiant ingenue falling in love for the first, delirious time. She didn't want to like it—but she couldn't help herself. She closed her eyes to hear it better.

The music swelled to its rhapsodic climax, and with it came a shift in the air, a delicate stirring that made the hair on Deal's neck rise. She could sense someone new in the room, could hear a high soprano hum floating along with the song. Her hands got cold. The floor felt unsteady. No! Not again, she nearly yelled. Get me out of here. Now! Her eyes snapped open. The song and the hum stopped, the last note hanging in the air. Mr. Ferrara and Laurie were both looking at her. She stared past them. No one else was there.

"It's called 'All the Things You Are,' " said Mr. Ferrara. "Did you like it?"

Deal let out an uncomfortable laugh. Babe, you are one easy mark. Somebody pulls a weird joke on you one day, and the next you're still falling for it. "It was . . . enchanting," she said.

"Good," said Mr. Ferrara. "Because you and Laurie will be singing it at our spring recital—"

"Great!" Laurie exclaimed.

"But—" Deal began.

Mr. Ferrara raised his hand. "Yes, I know you just joined the glee club, but I believe you have the best voice for this piece. That's not flattery, Delia. I never flatter."

"But," Deal repeated, "what if I say no?"

From the corner of her eye she saw Laurie's face fall. Mr. Ferrara kept his carefully neutral. "Is that what you're saying?"

"Not yet. I'd like to think about it."

"Fine. You can give me your answer after school. . . . Here's your pass."

Deal nodded and took it. She was halfway down the hall when Laurie caught up with her.

"Okay. I give up," he said. When she didn't reply he went on, "Why don't you want to do the duet?"

"I didn't say I didn't want to do it."

"No, but you're going to, aren't you?"

Deal shrugged. "I prefer being asked if I want to do something, not being told I'm doing it."

Laurie studied her for a moment. He shook his head. "That's not it, is it? Not all of it."

"What do you mean?" Deal said coolly.

"It's me, isn't it? You don't want to sing with me." He looked hurt.

She raised her eyebrows. Oddly enough, the thought hadn't occurred to her at all. She was surprised it had occurred to him. She thought he was more thick-skinned, more resilient than that.

"No. That's not it," she said.

"It isn't?"

"No . . ." She had a flash of her dream from last night,

the part before it went bad—she and Laurie doing a tap dance on a baby grand—and suddenly she wanted to reassure him. "Cross my heart and hope to die," she said, in a little-kid voice. He smiled. She did, too.

Then he asked, "If it isn't me, what is it, then?"

She stopped smiling. What could she tell him? That it wasn't the duet she wanted to avoid, but the room? That, practical joke or not, the place gave her the creeps and she didn't want to spend any more time there than she had to?

You're losing it, girl. Really losing it. Get it together. Right now. And get to the bottom of this. Her head suddenly cleared. "It was what I said. Mr. Ferrara bugged me. I just wanted to let him stew in his own juices," she said.

"So you really are going to do the duet after all?" Laurie said. He was trying to sound impassive, but hope was trembling in his voice. "You're really going to sing with me?"

Say no.

She paused, remembering his glorious tenor, and got a whiff of him. He smelled like apple soap, which struck her as exactly right. What if I don't want to? she told the voice in her head.

Then you lose one turn.

It was bad to waste time when she played the Game. Deal knew that. It doesn't matter. I'll still win. She squared her shoulders. "Sure," she told Laurie. "Why not?"

"Yowza!" he yelled and hugged her. Then he ran down the hall and crashed into a hall monitor. He waved a pass at her, as she bawled him out, and barreled on.

Do not pass go. Do not collect two hundred dollars.

Shut up, she replied, and sauntered on to class.

"What did Ferrara want with you and Sue?" Carter asked.

It was lunchtime, and Deal was starved. She swallowed a bite of pizza. "I thought his name was Laurie," she said casually, as if she didn't quite know and certainly didn't care.

"Laurie, Sue, they're all girls' names." Carter bit into his ham sandwich. Mustard oozed out onto the table.

"You're a pig, Carter. In more ways than one," Jean said, handing him a napkin.

"What *did* Ferrara want?" asked Tina. She was standing up, leaning against Mark and feeding him potato chips. Like a baby, he docilely opened his mouth for each morsel, while his eyes drifted around the room. That was fast, Deal thought, wondering when they'd had time to make up.

"We're doing a duet for the spring concert, Laurie and I," Deal said.

"A love song?" Tina's eyes widened.

"You could call it that."

"Ooh la la," said Carter. "Beauty and the Least."

Everyone laughed except Mark. "Look, there's Benson."

Deal turned to see the custodian, a fluorescent light-bulb in one hand, surveying the room. He nodded at her. She turned away, hoping no one else had noticed.

Mark was frowning. "Two months, and the guy still hasn't fixed those corroded taps in the showers."

"Yeah. Why don't they get rid of him? He's too old to cut it," said Carter.

"He's not that old. I bet he's not even sixty," said Tina. "And if they fired him, where would he get another job?"

"Hey, you were complaining just the other day about how the guys stink after practice and how those showers ought to be fixed, and now you're sticking up for the guy," Mark said irritably.

Tina glared at him.

It looked as if they might start arguing again, but it was, of all people, Deal who stopped it. "I heard that Al Benson saw the Brain Rot ghost," she said.

"Right. Through the bottom of a bottle," said Jean, swigging an imaginary fifth of Scotch.

"I don't think Benson drinks," said Mitch.

"How do you know?" asked Mark.

"Because my uncle does, and I know the signs," he replied, which shut everyone up.

"Maybe somebody was playing a trick on him," said Deal after a moment.

"Maybe someone *ought* to play a trick on him," said Carter.

Deal turned to him like a detective about to get a confession from a suspect. "How would you do it?" she asked.

Carter grinned crookedly. "Why? You want to be my partner in crime? Have someone dress up in white, I guess, play spooky sounds on a tape recorder, something like that."

"Mirrors," said Jean. "I'd do it with mirrors."

"What?" said Mitch.

"Isn't that how magicians do it? With mirrors?"

"Yeah—and with talent," said Carter.

"Ho ho."

"I don't like this discussion," said Tina. "I don't believe in playing tricks on people."

"Don't worry about it, Teen," Mark assured. "Nobody here is going to play any tricks. Nobody could anyway—unless they had a hologram or two."

"Why not?" asked Deal.

"Because Benson may be slow, but he's not stupid—he's not going to believe a kid in a white sheet is a ghost. Nobody would. Kids are solid. Ghosts are not."

White, she was, and wavery. And behind her, Deal had seen Mr. Ferrara's desk. No, not behind her.

Through her. But that was impossible. Impossible! I won't believe it. I can't, Deal thought. What was it Carter had said? If ghosts were real, why not angels or demons or aliens from space? What other nonsense would she have to accept? What things beyond her control? The list was endless, and endlessly disturbing.

"Ghosts aren't anything," Deal said, looking down at her half-eaten pizza. "They don't exist." Rising slowly, she carried her tray to the waste bin and pitched in the rest of her lunch.

chapter nine

S he told herself it was for the "dossier" she was com-
piling on Gram, that seeing someone where she
worked gave you all sorts of useful information about
that person. She didn't admit that this afternoon she
didn't feel like going home to an empty house.

The bus bumped and huffed along Cole Street. Two
more stops, Deal noted. She looked out the window. It
was snowing—it was always snowing these days. " 'You
are the promised kiss of springtime/that makes the
lonely winter seem long.' " She breathed the words—so
sappy, so haunting—without knowing for a moment
where they'd come from. Then she remembered. They
were from the duet.

When Deal, accompanied by Laurie, who'd probably
wanted to make sure she wasn't going to back out, told
Mr. Ferrara she'd do the duet, the teacher had called a
rehearsal on the spot. It hadn't been so bad, really. Actually, it had been pretty good, although she'd kept her

eyes open the whole time and twitched once when a poster suddenly fell off the wall. Mr. Ferrara was right about her voice being suited to the song. Her voice and Laurie's. They blended beautifully. "Sounding good, Partner," he said, using his new nickname for her. "Like larynxes in love."

"Give me a break," Deal had tried to jeer, but she laughed instead.

Renee will get a kick out of me singing, Deal thought, leaning against the bus window. I'll have to tell her about it. And about the ghost. She'll be *convinced* it's the real thing. Then Deal realized she hadn't heard from her mother in days, not by phone, not even by postcard.

"Oh, Deal," she could imagine Renee saying when she finally called. "I'm so sorry, but I've been *so* busy. Do you know how hard it is to get used to a new place? To live with someone"—her voice would drop to a whisper—"who leaves the toilet seat *up!*"

"No, Renee," Deal would reply. "I *don't* know how hard it is to leave your old home, city, state, and live with someone who leaves the toilet *lid down.* I don't know at all."

"Oh, baby. I'm sorry. I made you leave your home and all your friends, didn't I? I'm so selfish, aren't I?" Renee would get all contrite and weepy and talk about missing her daughter for about thirty seconds, and Deal would buy it for about thirty seconds. Then, with one of her split-second changes of mood, Renee would say brightly,

"Oh, well. No use fretting. We've got to make the best of things," and she'd go back to talking about Clark and her new apartment and her new job, etc., etc., and Deal would let her, just to hear her voice, until she ran out of steam. "Good-bye, baby. Oh, I do miss you so," Renee would say with a breathy flourish, and abruptly she'd be gone, leaving Deal holding on to the receiver with the irrational hope that her mother might just as suddenly reappear.

Maybe it's good I haven't heard from Renee, Deal thought, knowing she didn't believe it. She rubbed her eyes. They felt strangely gritty. She looked out the window again. The bus had stopped. She glanced at the street signs, then realized this was where she had to get off. The bus doors closed with a steamy wheeze. "Wait!" Deal called, hustling down the aisle. The driver tsked at her and let her out.

Fiorillo's Pharmacy was only a few blocks away, a fact which Deal appreciated. Her skirt was short and the cold wind slapped at her legs. The drugstore had recently been renovated. The wooden shelves had been replaced by multicolored pastel metal ones. Instead of the old prints of bearded doctors ministering to the sick, there were assorted advertisements for Band-Aids, cold remedies, dental floss, and the like. The chairs with peeling cushions where people once waited for prescriptions had been exchanged for ones of molded plastic in colors to match the shelves. Deal had visited here once before, a long time ago. The place had never been what she thought of as charming, but at least it had had character.

Gram, looking professional in a white lab coat, was handing an elderly man a prescription bottle. "Take one directly before each meal," she was saying.

"Eh?" the man asked. He was wearing a frayed coat missing several buttons.

"One before each meal," Gram repeated, louder.

"Gotcha," the man said. He took the bottle and began to head out of the shop.

"Mr. Glassner!"

He turned back.

"You forgot to pay me."

"Did I?" He reached into his pocket and took out a very old, very stained change purse, laboriously extracted two bills and a large number of coins from it, and put them on the counter in front of Gram.

"Another dollar, Mr. Glassner," she said calmly.

Deal fidgeted while the man dug out several more coins. Why didn't Gram just let him go?

"Thank you, Mr. Glassner," she said.

He grunted and shuffled toward the exit. "Could you get that door for me, girlie?" he asked Deal without looking at her. He reeked of heavy cologne.

Deal didn't like his smell or being called "girlie," but she did what he asked.

"Seventeen dollars! Ridiculous," he humphed, shambling past her and out the door. A black Cadillac stood at the curb. It had been there when Deal had arrived. She'd idly wondered who owned it. The shabby old man flung open the rear door with surprising strength and disappeared into the car, which promptly drove away.

Deal let out a surprised snicker.

"Things aren't always what they seem, are they?" Gram said. "I'll bet you thought I was the stingy one."

Deal turned slowly, taking in her grandmother's amused expression. "Not really," she replied, although it was exactly what she had been thinking. Then she asked, "Who is he?"

"That was Mr. Glassner. He made a bundle in snow-blowers, if you can believe that, and he hates to part with any of it. He may not be the town's only miser, but he's the most famous." Gram rolled her shoulders the same way, Deal realized with a little start, that she herself did. "What brings you here today?" Gram asked. She didn't sound particularly happy—or, for that matter, unhappy—to see her.

Deal felt a pang of disappointment. On the bus she'd had little twinges of anticipation. Renee had always given her a big greeting whenever she'd dropped in unexpectedly at the office. "Look, everybody. It's my beautiful daughter," she'd say, or something like it. But Gram wasn't Renee. So what if we've been getting along better at home, Deal tweaked herself. What did you expect, trumpets and drums?

"I need a new lipstick," she answered.

"Ah . . . Carolyn can help you with that," Gram said, nodding at the plump woman with blue eyes and a good dye job who'd just emerged from the stock room.

"I certainly can," the woman said. "You must be Deal. My, how you've grown. Do you remember me at all? You must have been only five or six the last time you came here. Now you're in high school, aren't you?"

Deal nodded.

"My grandson goes there. Maybe you know him. Mark . . . Mark Chelsom. Very handsome and popular. He has a lovely girlfriend you might have met—Tina Tchelichev? In fact, they're having dinner at my house tonight."

"Yes. I think I know who he is," said Deal. She set her books on a chair. She hadn't felt like carrying her pack today.

"Old Brain Rot High." Carolyn sighed. "Don't look surprised—we called it that back when Maureen and I went there. The place is still the same, even if we aren't." She winked at Gram, who was crossing over to another counter, and laughed so heartily that Deal couldn't help grinning.

"Say, if you ever want to see what your grandma looked like way back then, I've got our old yearbook at my house."

"Maybe I'll take you up on that sometime," Deal said.

The door opened then and two little boys raced in, followed by their harried-looking mother. "I need a home pregnancy test kit and a large bottle of aspirin," the woman said. "Jason, don't touch those!"

But the bigger of the boys had already seized Deal's books. His brother kicked him.

"Alex, no kicking! Jason, put those down!" their mother ordered.

Ignoring her, Jason took off around the room, followed by Alex. Their mother, a large woman, lumbered after them. Alex ran one way, Jason the other. Gram, on her way back to the high counter where she filled prescriptions, sidestepped him. He crashed right into Deal.

"Ouch!" she said as he connected with her belly. Her books fell to the floor. The motorcycle magazine spilled out from one of them to the floor. Deal didn't notice until Carolyn held it up.

"Oh, motorcycles. Are you interested in them, too? Mark's crazy about them."

"Is he?" said Deal, taking the magazine from her and tucking it back inside her book.

"That's what you get for not listening," Jason's mother scolded the crying boy, all the while rubbing his forehead. Alex stood by, picking his nose. Deal wanted to kick them both in the butts.

"Oh, yes. He wants to own some big monster of a machine—a Hadley or something," Carolyn went on.

"Really?" said Deal.

"Uh-huh . . . Now, what lipstick did you want?"

"Skip it. . . . You're busy now. I'll come back another time."

"Are you sure?"

"I'm sure," she said. She turned to go and saw Gram watching her. There was no warmth in her face—just something that looked like disapproval.

Sorry to interrupt your day, Deal thought. She gave Gram a sardonic smile and saluted.

Gram nodded curtly and returned to measuring out capsules.

Deal pushed open the door and headed straight for the nearest pay phone. She dialed the number she'd memorized. "Mark," she said when he answered the phone. "It's Deal. I thought you'd like your magazine back. My place or yours?"

"Nice place. Very neat." Mark said, surveying Gram's living room. He was an hour late. Royal Time, Deal supposed.

"Very, very neat," she agreed. "Do you want your magazine, a Coke, or both?"

"Both would be nice." Mark smiled. He settled down into the green sofa with an unself-conscious grace, as if he'd been there many times before.

Deal fetched the magazine and handed it to him. When she returned, he was staring at the picture of the Harley as though it were something holy.

"Which is it? The power or the freedom?" she asked, sitting next to him on the couch.

He looked up at her, understanding. "Both . . . and also how good I look in a helmet." He grinned.

"Yes. I'll bet you do." She gave a husky laugh.

He took a sip of Coke. "My oldest brother—he's got his own place now; I don't see him as much—but he's always had bikes. Used to give me rides. I thought that was Halo City until around last Turkey Time when he let me drive it myself. Then I found out what heaven was really like. . . ."

"What *is* it like?" Deal asked, leaning forward.

"What's it like . . . Humming down the highway, passing all those tin boxes on wheels—yeah, I know, I know; I've got one, and she's a nice old thing. She can move all right, but a bike can *travel*. On a bike, you can *feel* the road. You're part of it. You're in charge of it, in charge of not just your destination, but your destiny."

I wonder how often he's used that phrase before, Deal thought cynically. But the truth was that she was unexpectedly gripped by his description. "It does sound like heaven," she said.

"Yeah—God knows around this town there are few enough ways to get there."

"You've got more ways than most," Deal said.

"Yeah? Yeah, I guess I can't complain. Who'd believe me?" He gave an ironic laugh.

Poor thing, Deal thought, but she wasn't totally unsympathetic.

Then Mark said, "My brother said I can borrow his bike once in a while till I get my own. I'll take you riding sometime." It wasn't just an offer—it was a decree.

But Deal knew who was really in command. "I'd like that," she said softly, aware of how close together they were sitting. The air between them was full of unspoken words, like "Tina," "trouble," and "kiss."

Mark was aware, too. He took another sip of Coke. "I've got to go." He rose, not quite so graceful this time.

Deal walked him to the door. "I'm glad you came over," she said.

"Yeah," he answered.

She opened the door. Gram was standing there.

"Oh, hi," Deal said, momentarily flustered. "This is—"

"Hello, Mark," Gram said, and brushed past her granddaughter into the house.

"Ms. Murray!" Mark said, startled. "This is your granddaughter?" He looked at Deal.

"Didn't Carolyn tell you I had one?" Gram answered, coolly.

"I guess I didn't pay attention. I'm a lousy listener—Granca will tell you that."

"Granca?" Deal said, trying not to snicker.

"My brother, when he was little, couldn't say Grandma Carolyn," Mark explained. "It came out 'Granca.' Now we all call her that."

"Charming," said Gram, and Deal couldn't tell if she was being sarcastic or not.

"Well, I've got to go. Bye, Ms. Murray. See you around, Deal—and thanks." He tapped the magazine. Then, after taking the steps in one bound, he sprinted down the path and into his car and drove away.

Deal closed the door slowly, aware that Gram was still standing there in the narrow hallway.

"He came to get his magazine," Deal said. She felt defensive, and it bugged her.

"So I saw. The one 'Granca' asked about, wasn't it?"

Deal said nothing.

"The one she could have given him when he and his girlfriend come to dinner tonight."

"No," Deal replied, and wished she'd bitten her tongue.

"No? It looked like the same magazine to me."

"I meant no, Carolyn couldn't have given it to him with Tina there—she doesn't approve of his interest in motorcycles." Deal knew that the best course of action with Gram was to reveal as little as possible, but somehow, her grandmother had succeeded in throwing her off-guard and making her tell more than she should.

"And you do approve, I suppose."

"Yes, I do," Deal said, trying to sound offhanded.

"How kind of you. How understanding," Gram sneered. "So much more kind and understanding than Tina."

More kind and understanding than you, Deal wanted to fire back. "I've got homework to do," she said, trying to push past her grandmother.

But Gram blocked her path. "Be careful, Deal. Be very careful."

Deal stared at her until Gram moved aside. Then, silently, she strode to her room. Sitting on the bed, she swore steadily and quietly, inventing new and imaginative rude descriptions for her grandmother. The doorbell rang. Winston. Gram's date. She heard muted voices, waited until she heard the door slam.

Then she went to Gram's room. Throwing open the closet, she dug out the locked box and picked the lock with a pair of tweezers. A single, unsealed envelope lay inside, brown with age and handling. Without any hesitation, she opened it. Whatever she had expected, it wasn't this—a large, corny valentine with a big red rose on the front. Inside was an equally corny printed poem which didn't interest Deal at all. What did interest her was the message beneath, handwritten in cramped letters: "I'm so sorry. Marie."

Deal shivered. The card felt like a slab of ice in her hand, the cold shooting up her arm and down her spine. She got dizzy, as though her brain had slipped sideways. Something was wrong here. Why or what, she didn't know. Quickly, she shoved the card back into the envelope, the envelope into the box, and the box into the closet.

Shivering again, she went into the kitchen. She picked up the phone, put it back down, and picked it up again. Quickly she dialed Renee's number. The phone rang only once before an answering machine came on. She hung up without leaving a message. Crossing to the sink, she poured a glass of water and poured it back out, watching the water trickle down the drain.

A newspaper was lying open on the counter—a small sign of Gram's discomfiture. She never left newspapers lying open. Deal glanced at it. There was a big ad for Marco's Pizza. Deal grabbed the phone again. In a quavery, old-lady voice, she asked if that nice boy Laurie was delivering tonight.

"Yeah. Laurie's on," a hoarse male voice replied.

"Oh, thank you."

"You want to order?"

"No. Maybe next time," Deal told him and hung up. A moment later, she dialed again and in her own voice ordered a large pie.

"You picking up or you want that delivered?" the man asked.

"Delivered," said Deal. "And hurry."

chapter ten

———

Laurie's nose was dripping and his hands were red and so cold that Deal recoiled when she took the pizza box from him.

"Don't you have any gloves?" she asked.

"Lost 'em somewhere today, Partner," he said, pulling out a blue bandanna and blowing his nose. Who else would use a bandanna for a handkerchief? Deal thought.

He shivered a little. "Come in and warm up," she said.

"Thanks." His face lit up. Then, regretfully, he added, "I can't stay long, though. We're busy tonight." He followed her into the kitchen, babbling excitedly, nervously, all the while about order mix-ups and workers calling in sick.

Gram's perpetual pot of coffee sat in the coffeemaker. Deal poured a mug full and put it into the microwave. "Why do you use your bike for deliveries? Don't they have a car?" She was suddenly irked by his nerdiness.

Why had she ordered that pizza? Why had she sent for him?

"Yeah, they have a car, but the senior guy gets to drive it. He does the five-miles-and-over route. I do the town."

"That's ridiculous. They should have two cars, then."

"It wouldn't help me if they did. I don't have my license yet."

Deal didn't either, but that had never stopped her from driving Renee's Toyota every chance she got. What am I going to do with this guy? she wondered.

You don't have to do anything with him at all, said the voice in her head. *You're not his keeper.*

But I made him come here.

It's his job.

Sure. Riding a bike through a snowstorm to bring me a pizza I don't even want. Some job.

He could find another one if he wanted to.

Right, Deal agreed silently, but she wasn't sure. She'd never had a job herself but couldn't imagine they were so easy to come by. The microwave dinged. She took out the mug and handed it to Laurie.

"Thanks." He took it gratefully, warming his fingers on the ceramic.

She sat down at the table. He stood, looking around. "This place is so *neat,*" he said in amazement. "I feel like I should wash my pants before I sit down. . . . Oops." He was worried that he'd offended her.

But Deal laughed, a real laugh. "You should see the list

of rules Gram presented me with when I moved here—everything from sweeping up any crumbs from after-school snacks to not taking baths after ten P.M. My mother—" She stopped, a small cloud of sadness scudding across her face. "Renee never made rules," she finished.

"Is your mother still alive?" Laurie asked gently.

"Most definitely. 'The most alive she's ever been,' if you can believe her," Deal said acidly. When Laurie looked puzzled, she explained, "She's in St. Louis with her boyfriend."

"You didn't want to live with them?"

"They didn't want to live with me—and they were probably right. A couple of weeks with Clark and I'd end up on Oprah—'Teenage Girls Who Tried to Murder Their Mothers' Boyfriends.'" She laughed humorlessly, then carelessly added, "So here I am with Gram and her household rules." She shrugged as if it didn't matter.

Laurie let it pass. "My mother once *tried* to make a list of rules," he said. "But there are five of us kids. We argued over every one of them like a bunch of lawyers until Mom gave up."

Deal laughed again, and he sat down at last, grinning at her. Without thinking, she grabbed his mug and took a sip of his coffee as if it was the most natural thing in the world to do, as if they'd been friends for years.

"Do you like having brothers and sisters?" she asked.

"I don't know. I've never *not* had them." He smiled,

then continued. "I like them all most of the time. . . . But I don't have much privacy. We're always bumping into each other, barging in on each other's space, conversations, even thoughts. . . . Not like here. . . . Looks like you've got plenty of privacy. . . . You could keep secrets here."

"Secrets?" Deal said, seeing that lace-edged valentine hidden in its steel box. "Yes. This house keeps secrets." She reached for Laurie's mug again, hoping the coffee would get rid of the sudden chill she felt.

He waited for her to say more. When she didn't, he looked up at the clock, then at his hands. "I've got to go," he sighed. "You wouldn't happen to have a spare pair of gloves, would you? I could return them on Monday."

"I don't think so," Deal said distractedly.

"Oh, well. Thanks anyway—for the coffee and the, uh, thermal reprieve." He stood up. "Enjoy your pizza." He headed for the door.

"Hold it." Deal stopped him. "I've got something better than gloves."

"Mittens?" he said hopefully.

"No." She shook her head. "A car." It was Gram's, of course, but she wasn't using it—and with luck she'd never know that someone else had. "I'll help you deliver."

"Uh-uh. Driving's bad tonight."

"Bike riding's worse. And you'll have frostbite before

the night's through," Deal said, wondering why she was so insistent.

He hesitated another moment, then said, "Okay. But you'll have to take it slow."

"As slow as you like, Partner," Deal said. She took one more sip of coffee and led Laurie out of the room.

"Mr. Myers, now, he can eat a whole slice of pizza in one gulp. Mrs. Kornbluth, she eats pizza on her Nordic-Track. Joey Cremitone has to wear cowboy boots to eat pizza. Josie Cremitone has to wear a snood."

"A w-what?" Deal said, laughing. She'd been laughing for the past hour, it seemed, as they drove through the snow-covered streets, back and forth from Marco's, picking up and delivering pies. She didn't know whether half of what Laurie was saying was true, and she didn't care. He was entertaining—more entertaining than she could have imagined. He made her feel light, as if she'd just stripped off fifty pounds of armor.

"A snood," he repeated. "You know—one of those *Little Women*-ish hair-net things."

"Yeah? Does she also call her mother Mar-mee?" Deal asked, remembering something from a book she'd thought she'd forgotten.

"No. But Joey does."

Deal laughed again. "How about the people in there?" They were near the edge of town, the boundary of Laurie's route. There were fewer houses here, fewer lights. She pointed to an attractive home with two large spruce trees in the front. "How do they eat pizza?"

"You tell me," Laurie said lightly. "You know him better than I do. That's Mark Chelsom's house."

He knows, Deal realized. He couldn't have seen us together much—homeroom, English, that day after glee club. But he knows what I'm up to.

So what? said the voice in her head. *He doesn't count. He never will.*

"Ah, Mark. He can only eat pizza if it's served on a silver platter." Deal snickered, expecting Laurie to snicker, too.

But he didn't. Instead, he stared out the window and warned, "Be careful at this turning. There have been a lot of accidents here. A girl was even killed years ago. There used to be a marker for her—at least, that's what my mom said. Some people think that's who the ghost is."

"That ghost—I'm sick of hearing about her," Deal said irritably, speeding up just a little to scare him, just enough so that when the deer bounded in front of the car, she had to brake too hard and fast. The car fishtailed, avoiding a ditch, skidding nose-front into a snowbank.

Deal's nose bumped the steering wheel.

"Are you okay?" Laurie said, immediately unfastening his seat belt and Deal's, leaning over her.

"I'm fine," she said, refusing to rub her throbbing nose. "Are you all right?"

"I'll check. . . ." He patted himself exaggeratedly to make her laugh. She didn't. "Yeah, all there."

They sat silently for a moment. She wished he would put his arms around her. She wished he'd disappear. Then she said slowly, as if the words were being dragged out of her, "That was stupid of me. Really stupid."

He didn't disagree with her. "Do you think you can back out of here?" he said. "We ought to check the car for damage."

Deal nodded, reversing the automobile slowly, methodically. When she pulled it back far enough, she shut the engine, took a flashlight out of the glove compartment, and got out to survey the front end. It seemed unmarred. She glanced over at the road. Two feet to the left was the ditch.

"God," she said as the realization of how close a call it had been hit her. She shone the light into the hole. A small metal sign on a thin post lay in it three feet down, shining dully.

"That must be it," Laurie said.

She squatted and turned the flashlight beam on it. It was some sort of a sign. Squinting, she could only make out a few raised letters.

MARIE, they said. Underneath the name was a dark cross.

chapter eleven

D eal woke from a dream of ghosts rising out of ditches and tin boxes filled with valentines that turned into pulsating human hearts to the shrewish ringing of the doorbell. The sheet and blanket were all wrapped around her and she was glad no one was there to see her slapstick attempt at untangling herself.

Sweating from the nightmare and the exertion, she threw on her robe and stumbled to the door.

Tina, in a parka so white it hurt Deal's bleary eyes, was on the porch, along with Jean and a girl named Candy, another of the Sun King's court.

"Oh. You're not ready," Tina said.

"Ready for what?" Deal asked, too recently ripped out of REM sleep to be cautious or polite.

"You forgot, huh?" Tina chirped like a good-natured canary. Deal wanted to throw a cover over her. "You said you wanted to help with the valentines."

"What valentines?" Deal said, with sudden sharpness,

wisps of her bad dream drifting through her mind, making her shiver as much as the blast of cold air shooting through the open door did.

"Earth to Delia," said Jean.

Candy laughed.

"For the kids in the hospital. Don't you remember any of our conversation?"

"Maybe she was asleep then, too," Jean twitted.

"Right. The kids in the hospital," Deal said, not wanting to give them the satisfaction of knowing she really didn't remember at all. "Come in. I have to get dressed." She let them inside. "What time is it, anyway?"

"Ten," Tina replied. "Do you always sleep late, or did you have a big night?" She grinned, encouraging confidences.

"Big night," Deal replied, remembering her close call in the car. "Almost as big as eternity." The girls gave her puzzled looks as she left them in the kitchen.

Pulling on her clothes, she thought about last night. After their brush with disaster, she'd chauffeured Laurie around for another hour in a kind of daze. She wanted to talk about ghosts. She wanted to tell him about the card in the box. But she didn't. Instead, she grew more and more removed, wishing she hadn't gotten herself stuck with him for the evening.

She'd parked the car safely in the garage and herself safely in bed a half hour before Gram returned. Under the covers, listening to her grandmother padding quietly around the house, she realized she'd forgotten to put away the uneaten pizza and was sure to hear about it when the two of them saw each other again—which she hoped wouldn't be too soon.

In the kitchen, Tina and Candy were sitting at the table. Jean was examining the list of important numbers posted by the phone. No doubt searching for something worth gossiping about, thought Deal as she entered, knowing by Jean's guilty look she'd judged correctly.

"This place is so neat," Jean said.

"Actually, it's on the unkempt side today," said Deal. "When it's really neat, we don't allow anyone in for fear of messing it up."

Jean barked a laugh.

"I didn't know Ms. Murray was your grandmother," Tina said, changing the topic. "She works with Mark's grandmother at the drugstore," she explained to Jean and Candy. "She's the pharmacist."

"Really? Can she give me something to lose weight?" said Candy.

Deal didn't think she was joking.

"Carolyn showed us some old pictures of your grandmother last night. She looked just like you, Deal," said Tina. "Carolyn said they weren't in the same crowd, though."

"No. I can't imagine they were," said Deal.

"Why not?" Jean asked pointedly.

"I'm sure Gram's crowd was too sedate."

"Actually," Tina put in, "Carolyn said *her* crowd was."

"Really?" Deal couldn't disguise her surprise.

"Yes, she said your grandmother was the only girl she knew who drove a sports car and drank gin. And that she broke more than a few hearts."

"Sounds like your grandmother was kind of wild." Jean grinned.

"Sure," Deal said dryly, thinking of Gram's lackluster love life, her nondescript Subaru, and the lack of even a bottle of beer around the house. Maybe Carolyn's memory was failing. "A real rebelette."

Tina and Jean laughed. "Were you born to be wild, too?" Jean gibed. "You know, like grandmother, like granddaughter?"

"Not born—self-taught," Deal parried.

Tina and Jean laughed again.

"Or maybe she could give me some pills to make my boobs grow," said Candy, who'd obviously dropped out of the conversation some time back.

"I'll ask her," said Deal, deadpan.

"We ought to get going," said Tina.

"Actually . . ." Deal began, an excuse forming itself in her brain. She couldn't see herself spending the morning making valentines. She couldn't see spending it with these girls.

"Carolyn's waiting," Tina went on, not hearing.

"Carolyn?"

"She's in charge of the project—sucked us into it,

really. Good works don't come to me naturally." Tina laughed. There was that self-deprecating honesty again that Deal found hard to dislike.

Then the phone rang.

"Busy morning," Jean said.

"Hello," Deal said into the receiver.

"Ready for a trip to heaven?" the caller asked.

When Deal didn't reply, he went on, "It's Mark. My brother lent me his bike. We can take that ride."

Deal looked at the girls. Candy wasn't listening. Jean was pretending not to. But Tina was watching her with innocent, open curiosity. She smiled.

Deal smiled back.

"Hey, this *is* Deal, isn't it?" Mark asked.

"Yes," she responded at last. "It is."

"So, how about it?"

Not yet, said the voice. *Make him wait.*

"I'm busy today," she told him.

"Busy how?"

"Got plans with my friends Candy, Jean, and Tina."

There was a pause. "Is she there?" Mark asked.

"That's right," said Deal, enjoying his discomfort.

"Another time, then?"

"Another time."

Another pause. Then he said, "You won't tell her I called, will you?"

"Not unless you want me to," said Deal.

Mark laughed uncomfortably. "It can be our secret."

"I like secrets," said Deal.

Tina raised an eyebrow and winked.

Nice move, said the dry voice.

Thanks, she told it. She winked back at Tina. She'd never played the Game quite this way before. It gave her a kick—but left an odd aftertaste.

"See you," said Mark.

"Bye," said Deal, hanging up.

"Mr. Big Night?" asked Jean. "Or is that a secret, too?"

"I'll let you know if it is," Deal said.

"Cute," Jean retorted.

"Do you have any potato chips?" asked Candy. "I'll never make it to lunch."

"Sure," said Deal, taking out and tossing her the bag.

"Thanks. You're my friend for life."

"How nice," Deal said.

Carolyn's house couldn't, by any stretch of the imagination, be called neat. Books and magazines covered every available surface. Dried flower arrangements sprinkled crumbly petals on the carpet. Shoes and boots lay bunched in the front hall or askew near chairs and couches where Carolyn's feet had left them. In the kitchen, where she led them, a half-drunk cup of tea sat on a stepladder. A half-eaten doughnut teetered on the edge of the counter, next to a fat and sleepy longhaired tortoiseshell cat. The air was perfumed with a mixture of rose-scented bath oil and overripe bananas. It reminded

Deal of her old house, and it made her homesick and happy both at the same time.

Candy made for a box of crullers Carolyn offered. Tina and Jean began to sort out supplies that were on the table. Deal headed straight for the cat. "What's her name?" she asked. She'd had cats all her life. The last one had died in November. Renee had promised they'd get another one. That was two weeks before Clark had been given the boot by his wife and Deal had been given the boot by Renee. There was no use pressing for a new feline then—they both knew how Gram felt about cat hair.

"August. Bet you can't guess why," Carolyn said.

"You got her in August?"

"Aww. You guessed." Carolyn laughed.

"Hi, August. Who's a pretty, pretty girl?" Deal cooed, scratching that cat behind the ears. The car purred contentedly. She made Deal feel like purring, too.

"She likes you. That's a good sign," said Carolyn. "Maybe you'd like to take care of her when I go on vacation."

"Sure," Deal said, so enthusiastically that Jean looked over at her with amusement.

"I'd pay you, of course," Carolyn said.

Deal, who would have gladly paid Carolyn instead, nodded. "Of course," she said crisply.

"Terrific. We can work that out later. Now, I only have a little time today, so let's get to work."

Throughout the next hour, Deal drifted in and out of

the light conversation while her hands dipped, snipped, and sprinkled in a swirl of sequins, lace, glitter, glue, and construction paper. She felt like one of those women she'd seen pictures of in a history book at a quilting bee. How bored they must have been, she used to think. But now she wondered if maybe she was wrong. Perhaps they really enjoyed it, just the way she was actually enjoying the peaceful creativity of this arts and crafts session.

"To Lucy," she wrote with a gold glitter pen. "Happy Valentine's Day from Your Secret Friend." She checked off the girl's name from the list Carolyn had given her. One more name to go. Good. Despite the pleasantness of the work, she wanted to be finished. She was eager to see those photos of Gram.

"Darn. We're nearly out of glue," said Carolyn. "I thought I had enough. I'll just go down to the basement. I think Frank has some down there." She left hurriedly.

"Good. Almost done," Candy said, echoing Deal's thoughts. "Dave didn't believe me when I told him it wouldn't take long."

"How nice of him to let you off your chain for the morning," Jean said.

"Dave doesn't have me on a chain. I *like* to be with him. Just the way Tina likes to be with Mark."

"Yeah, but she doesn't have to ask his permission to do things without him."

"You mean to tell me he didn't mind even a teensy bit that you were hanging out with us this Saturday instead of with him?" asked Candy.

"No, he didn't. He thought it was a great idea," Tina, inscribing a card, replied serenely. "He had his own things to do."

"What things?" asked Jean.

"I didn't ask."

"I bet it has to do with M-blank-T-blank-R-CYCLES."

"No, it doesn't. He promised me last night he wouldn't ride them anymore," said Tina.

"And you believed him?" said Jean.

"Of course. A relationship has to be based on trust. Don't you think so, Deal?"

Deal was looking at August the cat through the slits in a doily. "Trust and the XY chromosome don't mix," she said.

"Huh?" said Candy.

Jean laughed. Tina shook her head. "I don't believe that. If I did, I couldn't love anyone, let alone Mark. . . . Oh, no!"

"What's wrong?" asked Jean.

"This was supposed to go to *Mary*." She held up the card she was working on. In beautiful curlicued letters she'd written, "To Mark."

"Don't worry. Make another one for Mary and give that to Mark for V-Day. It's prettier than a store-bought card," Candy said, with easy practicality.

"Yeah. Sign it from 'Your Secret Admirer' and slip it into his locker." Jean grinned.

"His *gym* locker." Candy grinned, too. "Don't you think, Deal?"

"Sure," Deal said. But she hadn't heard her. She was thinking about the card in the steel box. Why a valentine? she wondered. If Marie—the name gave her the shivers—was apologizing to Gram, wouldn't she have just written a note?

"Of course, Mark might not know it's from you," Jean teased Tina. "He's got to have at least three dozen other secret admirers."

"Definitely," said Candy. "Some of them are even prettier than you!"

"I hope they are," Tina joked back. "It would be embarrassing if they were uglier."

They laughed, and Deal joined in. But she was still thinking about the heart.

Carolyn returned a few moments later. They finished up the last few valentines. Then Deal said, "About those photos you have of Gram . . ."

"Oh, yes. In our yearbook . . . Let me get it. . . ." She disappeared for what seemed a long time, only to return empty-handed. "Would you believe I can't find it?" she moaned.

Yes, I would, thought Deal.

"I had it out just last night. I'm sorry, but I'm afraid I don't have time to poke around looking for it, either. . . .

I'm sure it'll show up, though. . . . Tell you what. When I find it, I'll give you a call."

"You don't have to do that. It's not important," Deal said. But it was—anything that provided a clue to Gram was significant.

"No, I will. . . . Now I've got to skedaddle. Thank you, girls, so much for your help. The children at St. Luke's will be so thrilled. If any of you want to help me deliver these next Saturday . . ."

"I will," said Tina.

"Me, too," Jean chimed in.

"So will I—that is, if I'm free," said Candy.

"That is, if Dave will let her," Jean teased.

Then they all looked at Deal.

"Sorry. I'll be busy," she said. She'd make sure of it.

chapter twelve

By the time Deal left the girls, who were gabbling excitedly about the evening's upcoming basketball game, it was midafternoon and she was laden with a bunch of small bundles, the results of a spontaneous shopping expedition. Unlike most girls she knew, Deal didn't much like shopping—except for flea markets. She'd said as much to Tina.

"Flea markets! There's a fabulous one out on Telmark Road. We can take the bus there."

Deal supposed she could have wiggled out of the trip, but the truth was she didn't have any other plans, and she wasn't totally bored with Tina and company's company. The excursion turned out to be more fun than she'd expected. On the bus ride, Tina, chairperson of the dance committee, initiated a game that Deal found entertaining about truly bad themes for the upcoming Valentine's Day dance. Which Jean won with "Come as Your Favorite Cannibal"; slogan: "Eat Your Heart Out." And the flea market *was* fabulous. Deal found, among other things, a book on the lore of flowers, guitar-pick earrings, and a tiny and very ugly porcelain cat figurine. She didn't need any of them, which made their purchase all the more pleasing.

Gram was still at work when she got home. But there was evidence that she'd returned for lunch. ("Why should I waste money on eating lunch out when I can zip home and make myself a perfectly good sandwich?" she'd told Deal a while back; Deal had chosen not to argue with her choice of the words "perfectly good.") The mail, which hadn't been there when Deal left, was now neatly stacked on the hall table. Two pieces were addressed to her—a postcard (at last) from Renee and a small padded envelope with no stamp or return address.

She read the postcard first. "My Dearest Only Girl Child," it began.

Oh, God. Deal winced. Renee in one of her overblown sentimental moods.

"I keep dreaming of you in pigtails and braces . . ."

"I never wore braces," Deal muttered.

". . . even though you didn't wear braces. I did. So who am I seeing? Me in you or you in me? A way to keep you close. Clark's new job is keeping him rather busy. I haven't had a good foot massage in weeks. I miss you ever so. Love, Mom."

"Me or my foot massages," Deal sneered, but her lip was trembling. I can't stand hearing from her and I can't stand not hearing from her. Her lip quivered again. Stop it! She pulled on it, hard. Stop it, stop it, stop it! Control's the key, Deal. Don't let anyone make you lose control.

She thought about burning the card, but shoved it into her jeans' pocket instead. Then she picked up the padded envelope and tore it open, shaking out a tape and a card. The latter was blue with a large white snowflake—the kind kids make in grade school—pasted to the front. It was clearly a handmade and hand-delivered job. Puzzled, Deal opened and read it.

"Thanks for saving me from frostbite last night. No s-kidding!" It was signed, "In your debt, Laurie." Beneath his cheerfully large signature was a P.S.: "Listen to this tape, especially Side 2. I found it at the flea market this morning."

Deal let out a snort. In my debt for what? Almost getting us killed? What a fool! Her lips twitched again—this time with amusement. "What a fool!" she repeated. Her voice sounded like she was talking to a cat.

She picked up the tape. "Broadway Show Stoppers," said the label. Without bothering to check the list of selections, she popped it into her Walkman. Most of the songs struck her as nice and quaint. Then came the final cut. The verse was different, but she recognized the tune at once. It was their duet. But comparing their version to this one was like comparing two pretty daisies in a glass to a lush bouquet in a crystal vase. The singers' voices soared and spiraled, weaving in and out of the full chorus with rich, complex harmony. Deal lay on her bed and played the song again and again, thrilling to the layers of sound, subtle and shifting as smoke.

At last she took off her earphones and sat up against her headboard. Her skin felt supple and her bones soft. The music had melted her.

When the phone rang, she rippled toward it like a skate fish gliding along the ocean floor.

"Deal, is that you? It's Laurie. Did you get the tape? Did you listen to it yet?" he burbled.

"Yes, I listened to it," she said, not giving anything away.

"Isn't it incredible?"

"It's pretty good."

"Pretty good? Are you trying for the Junior Achievement Award in understatement?"

She laughed. He'd done it again. Somehow he always managed to sneak past her guard right into her castle. No, that was wrong. He didn't sneak. He walked right up to the front door and knocked, and she let him in.

"Okay, okay," she said. "It's gorgeous. . . . *Too* gorgeous. We could never sound like that, Laurie."

"Of course not. They're them and we're us, Partner."

"That's not what I mean. . . . They sound . . . like they know what love is," she finished.

"Don't you?"

"No," she said, understanding all at once why people could tell intimate secrets on the phone they wouldn't dare reveal in person. "I don't."

"I can't believe that," Laurie said.

"Why not? It's true. I've never been in love, so how could I know what love means?"

"I think you can know what you're looking for even if you haven't found it yet."

"Who says I'm looking for it?"

"Because everyone is," Laurie answered simply. "One way or another."

Not me, Deal thought. Love is a mirage. It was a sentiment she'd repeated to herself many times before. But this time the words sounded hollow.

After a moment, Laurie said, "So, are you going to the big game tonight?"

She hadn't really thought about it. She didn't care about basketball. But Mark would be playing. It would be nice to see him in shorts. And she might be able to make another move in the Game. "Probably," she said. "You?"

"Gotta work. Don't worry, I got new gloves. Good ones. Insulated."

"I wasn't worrying," she said, not unkindly.

"Well, back to Pizzaland," he said.

"Okay. See you. Thanks for the tape."

"Mon plaisir," he said in good French and hung up.

Deal rose and stretched. She looked at her clock. Four-thirty. Plenty of time to make her escape before Gram came home. Then she looked at the clock again. Hadn't it said four-thirty when she'd started playing the tape? She picked it up. No ticking. The battery must have died. She hurried into the kitchen, where the clock read five forty-five. Oh no. Too late, she thought, just as she heard the garage door rumble shut.

Jump before you're pushed, Deal told herself. "Hello, Gram," she said, meeting her grandmother outside on the porch. "I was just leaving. I'm sorry about not putting away the pizza last night. I know it must have distressed you." Okay, Gram. Deal braced herself. Now take your best shot.

"Would you like some dinner before you go? I've bought Chinese food," Gram replied.

"What?" Deal asked, thinking perhaps she hadn't heard right.

"Vegetable dumplings and General Tso's chicken," Gram answered, misunderstanding the question. "You do like Chinese food, don't you? Renee always did, so I thought you might, too."

Was this a trick? Deal scrutinized Gram for signs of deception. "Yes, I like it," she said cautiously.

Gram nodded. "Then can you stay for dinner? We didn't see much of each other last night. I think it would be nice to spend time together this evening."

Maybe it was a peace offering. Deal wondered briefly if she should accept it. Then she caught a whiff of the food and her stomach rumbled. When had she eaten last? She wasn't good at keeping track. "Yes, I can stay," she said.

"Good. You set the table and I'll dish up the food."

"How was your date last night?" Deal asked, a short while later, as she deftly speared a chunk of chicken with chopsticks.

"Fine," Gram said, without elaborating.

"Are you going to see him again?"

"Perhaps."

Is he a good kisser? Does he have a cute butt? Is he rich? Deal reeled off questions in her head. "What do you like best about him so far?" she finally asked, wondering how Gram would evade that.

But instead Gram smiled. "His honesty. An important trait, don't you think?"

"Definitely," Deal said with exaggerated emphasis. "On a scale of one hundred, I'd say honesty is . . . there somewhere."

If she'd hoped to irk Gram, she'd failed. "You would say something like that, wouldn't you?" Gram said, knowingly. And it was Deal who got annoyed. She didn't want to be thought of as predictable. Then Gram asked, "Where are you going tonight?"

"To the game," Deal said.

"Really? I didn't know you were a basketball fan. . . . Perhaps I'll come, too. I love the sport."

Deal was dumbstruck.

"Don't look so horrified. I won't sit with you if you don't want me to," Gram said stiffly.

"No, it's okay," Deal said. "If you want to sit with me, that would be okay."

Gram nodded. "Well," she said briskly. "Well, we'd better eat up, then, and get going."

They finished the meal quickly. Gram seemed almost buoyant as she went to get a sweater. Her good mood was contagious. Deal washed the few dishes with extra elbow grease, singing as she did: " 'Someday my happy arms will hold you/Someday I'll know that moment divine/When all the things you are are mine . . .' "

Suddenly behind her she heard a gasp. She spun around.

Gram, never ruddy to begin with, had gone the color of birch bark.

"Gram! What's wrong?" Deal exclaimed, a list of terrifying medical possibilities ripping through her mind.

"Why are you singing that?" Gram demanded. "Who told you to sing that?"

"Mr. Ferrara did. The glee club director. It's a duet I'm doing with a kid named Laurie, for the spring concert," Deal answered, too confused to do other than tell the truth.

"You . . . you didn't ask my permission to be in glee club."

Deal stared at her grandmother in disbelief. Part of her

sensed that that wasn't what Gram wanted to say. The other part was outraged at her for saying it. "Since when do I need your permission for *anything*, never mind glee club?"

"I'm your *grandmother*."

"Then *act* like it," Deal spat.

"What's that supposed to mean?" Gram rapped out.

Hug me! Show me how glad you are that I'm here, Deal wanted to shout. Love me, damn it! Love me. She glared at her grandmother and saw that though her lips were pursed, her eyes were haunted. Some of Deal's anger faded. What's going on, Gram? What happened to you to make you like this? she wondered. "I'm going to the game," she said, wiping her hands on the dish towel. "You still want to come?"

"No . . . I don't think so. I have a bit of a headache." Gram's eyes had gone sad now, with a burden Deal could not understand. "Don't come home too late," she added, grandmother-like.

"I won't," Deal answered. If I come home at all.

chapter thirteen

"I *saw* it, I tell you! I saw it, and so did Jenny, Kelly, Laura, Keene, Joanne, and I don't even know who else." Clutching her coat over her short blue and gold uniform, the cheerleader from Moore High, Brain Rot's arch rival, waved her cigarette for emphasis. "I saw the ghost!"

"Sure you did, Bonnie," said her friend, plucking the cigarette from her hand and taking a drag. She pulled her coat closer, too. "Hurry up with this thing, will you?" she said, handing back the butt. "It's freezing out here." She gestured to the parking lot. Brain Rot students hurried past them, eager for the battle of the two best teams to begin.

The girls ignored them, as well as another student who was leaning against the wall nearby, tying her shoe and listening to every word they said.

"It was all white and fluttery. And it had this breathless voice like . . . like . . ."

"It was having an asthma attack?"

"No. Like it had traveled a long way from . . . the Other Side."

Her friend snorted.

How gullible, Deal thought as she worked on her second shoe, which didn't really need tying. But her conviction was not as wholehearted as she wanted it to be.

"I don't know why you won't believe me—us. Everybody saw it but you, Wendy. It was right over there— behind those trees." She pointed to the wooded area across the lot. Across from Room 513.

"I didn't say I didn't believe *you*." The girl called Wendy tossed her hair back.

"Then what?"

"I don't believe *it*. Somebody was pulling your leg."

"No. It was too real for that."

Wendy sighed. "Whatever. You have to forget about it now. We all have to forget about it. We've got a game to play. . . . Dev-ils! Dev-ils!" she began to cheer. "Go, Devils, go."

"Dev-ils," the other girl, Bonnie, chimed in. "Dev-ils! Go! Fight! Win!" She leaped in the air.

"Boo! Hack 'em! Boo! Whack 'em!" yelled some Brain Rot students passing by. They charged at the cheerleaders, who ran, squealing, into the school.

Deal stood up, hugging the shadows, staring out at the woods. She couldn't see anything but the massed forms of the trees. The crowds of students passing by had thinned to a few stragglers. Despite the cold, she waited until they, too, were gone, her eyes straining to see— what? Was that a flicker or a shimmer? Did she see a streak of light?

This is ridiculous, Deal told herself. You can find better ways to waste your time. She turned to go, then looked back briefly once more.

Something white and wavery was coming out of the woods. Deal inhaled sharply. Somewhere behind her, a window snapped open a crack. She clapped her hand over her mouth so she wouldn't scream. The white shape came closer. It spoke: "Hal, hurry up, will you? This thing's bulky."

Deal dropped her hand. The figure was close enough to see now. It was a guy carrying a bunch of fabric, ropes, and some kind of spotlight. Another guy followed behind with some more equipment. A tape recorder, Deal guessed.

"Carter owes us," said Hal.

"The whole team owes us!" said the first boy. His voice was familiar. Deal thought he might be a guy named George from her science class.

Then he saw her. "Uh-oh. Friend or foe?"

"Friend," she replied.

"Did you see it? Did you see our ghost?"

"Yes. I saw it," she answered. "You did a good job."

"Yeah. Well, the woods helped."

"Was Carter in on it last time, too?" she asked casually.

"Last time?"

"Hey, quit jawing and let's go. I want to see the game," said the third confederate.

"Yeah, okay." The boy who'd been talking to Deal hoisted the light up to the window, where the third boy lifted it through. The rest of the equipment joined it, followed by the two other guys. The window snapped shut.

The mystery is solved. So much for ghosts, Deal told herself. Briskly she left the shadows and silence of the parking lot for the glare and hubbub of the gym.

The bleachers were sagging with spectators. Everyone had turned out for this particular game. Everywhere Deal glanced there was someone she recognized vaguely or well from school or town. There was Mr. Walters sitting with Mr. Medgers, the principal, a former basketball player himself, who'd promised to lead his students on a run through their hallowed halls if the Shooters beat the Devils. In another section Carolyn and her husband, Frank, were clustered near a handsome couple who could only be Mark's parents. They were all applauding Tina, Jean, Candy, and the other cheerleaders, who were rousing the audience with pyramids, basket tosses, double twists, and short skirts.

Deal was gripped by a sense of not belonging. The crowd was vibrating like a giant violin to its own excited music. It jangled her ears. She looked around for a place to sit and found a spot at last between a very large boy and a very small one. Her mouth was dry. She licked her lips and thought they tasted like pizza. She wondered if that was how Laurie's tasted. She wished he were here. Or that she wasn't. Taking out her Walkman, she jammed on her earphones and listened to the tape he'd given her until Mark, Carter, Mitch, and the other players ran out on the floor and the game began.

Deal didn't know (or care) much about basketball, but she didn't find it hard to follow. When the Brain Rot fans cheered, it meant something good had happened to the Shooters. When Moore High cheered, it meant the reverse. And Mark—the golden, beautiful Sun King, all grace and speed—seemed always to be at the center of it all.

At the top of his game. The phrase floated out of nowhere into Deal's head. She thought of a story they'd read in English last year. It was about a strange bookstore where people could picture through a magic book the high point of their lives. For some of them it had yet to come. For some it was already past. Like the narrator. He learned that the high point of his life had happened when he was ten and he caught a fly ball to win the game. Nothing to come would ever match that moment, that pinnacle. The knowledge made him so depressed he nearly wanted to die. Deal wondered if now was Mark's high point. She wondered if getting Mark was hers. Her crowning achievement. Would she look back years from now and even remember him? Would it matter if she did?

All around her fans were chanting, shouting, rising. She rose with them and looked at the scoreboard. Sixty-eight to sixty-six. Two minutes to go. She stared at Mark racing across the court, at Tina, with her shining face, doing handsprings on the sidelines. Tina, who loved Mark, or at least thought she did. Suddenly aching for them all, Deal felt a great surge of shame and disgust. She wanted to leave before the crush, before the dizzying victory celebration or the wearing comedown of defeat, before she had to make another move in her own game. She started down the bleachers.

Quitter, said the voice in her head.

A quitter is someone who leaves when she's losing. I'm not losing, Deal answered it.

You're losing, all right. You're losing your nerve.

I don't have to listen to you. I don't have to do this.

Don't you?

The words seemed to hang in the air, suspending Deal in midmotion.

"Stay or go, but get out of my way," complained a scrawny guy, chomping on an unlit cigar.

Deal listed intentionally, knocking the stogie from his mouth.

"Hey!" he yelled.

"Sorry," she muttered and climbed back to her seat.

The fat boy next to her gave her a strange look. She ignored him and turned on her Walkman, letting the music become an oddly appropriate sound track to the dancelike game going on below.

The score tied, untied, and tied again. Mark, who before could do no wrong, suddenly could do nothing at all. Two minutes, Deal realized, could be an eternity. Two minutes could be the difference between yes and no. She supposed that that idea contained a useful lesson of some sort.

The clock ran out, and they went into overtime. The crowd was in a fever. Deal wondered if the bleachers were going to collapse, if the gym itself might burst like a sun going nova. But it was Mark who burst—up and up into the air, as though his high-tops had wings.

The crowd, Deal with it, held its breath as the ball kissed the rim of the hoop. The buzzer sounded. When it sank in, almost daintily, there was a moment—just the merest beat—of collective silence before everyone went wild, stomping and screaming. The cheerleaders spun and somersaulted. The Shooters hoisted Mark up and carried him around the court, then hustled out to the safety of the locker room.

With the team gone, the fans swept down and out into the hall, taking Deal with them. Joined by the cheer-leaders, they were met by Mr. Medgers and several burly security guards, who began to lead the lap around the school. Struggling against the flow, Deal ducked into the first doorway she came to and huddled there, catching her breath, watching the crowd press by.

She was still there when the players began to emerge from the locker room into the now-empty corridor. They sauntered out in twos and threes, their valentine red jackets pulsing in the harsh fluorescent light. Tonight they owned the school, the town, the world.

"Congratulations, Mark," Deal said as he appeared with Carter.

He turned regally—the king about to bestow a wave to a subject—until he realized who had spoken. "Deal!" he said, unguarded, boyish.

Get him alone, said the voice in her head.

Where? she asked it.

Try the door.

She smiled and turned the knob. The door swung open. She beckoned Mark inside.

"Catch you in five," he said. Deal caught a glimpse of Carter's smirk as Mark followed her into the room.

The piano hulked dark and large in the middle of the floor. Deal stood near it. Even through the closed windows they could hear the crowd in the parking lot cheering lustily as the players emerged. "Shoot-ers! Shoot-ers!" they yelled.

"I'm sorry I couldn't take that trip to heaven this afternoon," Deal said.

He laughed, low. "How about taking it now?" he said, and he kissed her.

The line was absurd, the kiss too hard. But she didn't pull away.

"Shoot-ers! Shoot-ers! Chel-som! Chel-som! We want Chelsom!" the crowd chanted.

"Your public awaits," she said when they broke apart.

"Let them wait," he said. He played with a lock of her hair. "You're beautiful, you know that?"

"You can't see me in the dark."

"I can see you with my eyes closed. You're not like any girl I've ever met. . . . You could break my heart."

"Yes, I could," Deal murmured. She wasn't sure he'd heard her—or if she'd wanted him to.

"Chel-som! Chel-som!" hollered the crowd.

"You'd better go," Deal said.

"Yeah . . . When can I see you again?"

"Monday. In school."

"I meant, when can I see you alone?"

"That's up to you," Deal said, although it wasn't.

"Chel-som! Chel-som!"

He kissed her again, quickly this time. Then he tugged at the bottom of his jacket and left.

Congratulations, said the voice in her head. *I wasn't sure you still had the talent.*

Then you don't know me, do you, she sneered back. She wiped her mouth and waited, allowing Mark a head start. Then she made for the door. Her hand was on the knob when she felt a sudden chill on her spine.

"Delia. Oh, Delia," whispered a mournful voice behind her.

Her breath clutched in her throat. She let it out. "Cut it out, George," she rasped. "You and your buddies, you're not funny!"

"De-li-a," the sad voice sighed. It sounded like it wanted to give her something—or take it away.

"I said stop it! You've been exposed, Lady in White. You're a hoax!" she declared. "Nothing but a hoax! You have no power over me!" With forced slowness, she opened the door. She didn't look behind her as she strode out of the room.

chapter fourteen

The bathroom floor chilled her feet. She didn't care. At least it took her mind off the dream. For a person not prone to nightmares, Deal was having more than her fair share lately.

This one hadn't started off badly. She was wandering in the woods, lost but not frightened, when she came upon a small house. The door was open. The one large room was warm, cozy. A fire burned in the grate. A cat snoozed by the fire. Deal went to pet it, and somehow she turned into the cat. Someone was petting her. She couldn't see who it was, but the touch was gentle, re-assuring. She purred.

Then everything changed. The room went cold and angular. A hazy white shape appeared. "Delia. Oh, Delia," it sobbed. The shape came closer. "Delia! Deal!" it snarled. It rushed her like a tidal wave, pinning, drowning her.

She tried to scream and couldn't. Which was just as

well. If she had, it would have pierced not only the dream, but the bedroom walls, waking Gram, demanding an explanation.

She shifted on the toilet lid and eyed the tub. She wanted a hot bath. But it was out of the question, according to the Household Rules. Then she heard footsteps. Damn. She'd awakened Gram, anyway.

Her grandmother knocked on the door and then, when Deal didn't answer, opened it and looked in. "What are you doing in here?" she croaked.

"Reading," Deal said.

Gram nodded, as if the explanation made sense. She came in and opened the medicine cabinet.

"I'm sorry I woke you," Deal said.

"You didn't." Gram sneezed. "I appear to be coming down with something." She shook a couple of pills out of a bottle and downed them.

"Really?" Renee, who got sick with every change of season, had once bemoaned the fact that her constitution wasn't as strong as Gram's. "Maybe it's not your constitution," Deal had replied. "Maybe it's just that germs don't like cold-blooded animals." "That's mean," Renee had said. But she'd laughed.

"So, I take it we won the game," Gram said, leaning against the sink.

"Yes, we won."

"Good." She sneezed again. She blew her nose and

rubbed her temples. "I'm going back to bed. A hot bath is good when you can't sleep," she called over her shoulder.

"Oh. You mean I have your permission to take one?" Deal said. It was a rabbit punch, and she knew it—bringing up their earlier argument, maybe starting another one.

Gram was either too charitable or too sick to fight back. "Just rinse out the tub after," she said.

"Yes, ma'am," Deal replied, turning on the taps.

The bath helped her sleep—but not well. She awoke late and unrested, expecting Gram to mock her laziness. She herself always rose early, even on her days off. "Otherwise I'll turn into a real slugabed," she liked to say, raising in Deal's head images of fat speckled mollusks immobile on flowered quilts.

So Deal was startled to discover that her grandmother was still in bed. Opening the door carefully, Deal peeked in on her. She looked pale against the pillows, except for her nose, which was red and raw. She really *is* sick, Deal realized. Instead of pleasing her, this evidence of Gram's vulnerability made her nervous. Closing the door, she pattered to the kitchen. What am I going to do today? she asked herself.

I could call Mark. No, the timing isn't right. She didn't want to see Tina or the other girls. What, then? She wondered what Laurie was doing. She jumped when the phone rang.

"Do you think there really is a 'special providence in the fall of a sparrow'?"

"What?"

"Providence—design. You know, like nothing ever happens by accident. Everything's fated. You can maybe escape things for a while. But sooner or later, your fate catches up to you."

"Laurie, what are you talking about?"

"*Hamlet*, Act Five, Scene Two."

"We're only on Act Two."

"I like to read ahead. Anyway, do you think it's true?"

"No," said Deal. "I don't believe in fate. I think plenty of things happen by accident. Don't you?"

"I don't know. Sometimes I think there is some Grand Scheme. Sometimes I don't."

"I hope you weren't up all night thinking about this." Deal stifled a yawn.

"Not *all* night." She could hear him grinning. "So, do you have any plans today?"

"I always have plans . . ." she said dryly.

"Oh." He sounded disappointed.

"But I don't always act on them," she finished.

"Oh. Well. Then do you want to maybe practice today?"

"It's Sunday."

"I know. I've got the day off. The whole blessed day."

"Laurie, Sunday means the school's closed, remember? No school, no music room."

"Yeah, but we've got a piano."

It sunk in slowly that he was inviting her to his house, and even more slowly that she actually wanted to see it—and him.

"Okay," she said. "We'll practice."

"Great!" he said, and hung up. Ten seconds later he called again to give her his address. "See you in half an hour—that is, if you make the 12:06 bus."

"I'll make it if you let me off the phone," said Deal, laughing.

"Okay, okay, I'm going. Hear me go."

She smiled all the way to the bus stop.

Everyone in Laurie's house seemed to be in perpetual motion, from his younger brothers wrestling on the floor to his sisters, one doing handstands, the other practicing tricks with their bouncy dog, to his mother, a very small woman, moving furniture with the strength of a construction worker.

Laurie rattled off their names, finishing the intros with "Everybody, this is Deal."

"That's your name?" said one of the brothers.

"It's weird," said the other.

"We're sending them off to charm school soon—or maybe out to sea," said Laurie.

They jumped on his back. He shook them off as if they

were nothing but pesky flies. They landed on the carpet, and the dog, completing a jump over the coffee table, landed on them.

Deal tried to imagine herself living in such friendly chaos and failed.

"Momster," Laurie asked, "Could you possibly accompany us on the Steinway?"

"Why, soi-tainly," said Mrs. Lorber, like one of the Three Stooges. Clearly Laurie was his mother's son, thought Deal. "After I finish this. In the meantime, why don't you offer Deal something to wet her whistle and show her around."

Laurie complied. Mugs of tea in hand, he and Deal strolled through the house with Laurie as tour guide. He pointed out "remarkable biographical artifacts," such as the butt-shaped candy dish he'd made in third grade, the chipped bathroom tile where he'd bumped his head at age nine after a never-repeated experiment with a bottle of Scotch, and the rubber plant still sparkling with the bagels and tinsel he'd decorated it with for Hanukkah. He was even funnier than he'd been on the pizza route the other night, and Deal told him he'd better end the tour or she'd be too hoarse from laughing to sing.

"Okay. Final stop," he said as they entered his room.

The walls were covered with shelves, the shelves with records, CDs, and tapes. Whatever space wasn't taken up by the collection was plastered with posters, prints, and magazine clippings of people, some famous, some not, all singing. She walked around, looking at them.

"You're serious about music, aren't you?" she said, sitting on the bed.

"Yeah. I'm serious." He leaned against his desk.

"You want to be famous?"

"I won't deny that it would be nice, but it's not my 'raison d'être.' If I make it to Carnegie Hall, great. If I make it to Manny's Supper Club, that'll be okay, too. I just want to keep singing. I'm going to study voice at some fabulous music college—Oberlin or Juilliard—and from there, I'll hit the road."

He sounded strong and determined—and he looked it as well. His eyes were luminous. His thin frame took on weight and substance. In ten seconds, he'd been transformed from a boy into a man—an extraordinary one. Deal felt stirred and unsettled.

"Yeah? I thought that nobody from around here ever leaves," she said, flicking a piece of lint off the quilt. She hoped he wouldn't ask about her plans. She had none, and for the first time that embarrassed her.

"*I'm* leaving," he said. "Want to come with me? We could be a duo."

There was no mistaking the earnestness in his tone. Yes, she almost said impetuously. Instead, she picked up a tape lying on his nightstand. It was by some old-time singer she'd never heard of. The first track was called "Taking a Chance on Love." She put it back down.

The silence was awkward. The bed felt strange, a place of previously unconsidered possibilities. Then Laurie asked lightly, "So, how was the game last night, Partner? We won, right?"

"Yeah. It was a cliff-hanger," Deal replied. She didn't like this kind of small talk.

"I heard that Mark Chelsom was the big hero."

"That's right. Mark and the ghost." It had slipped out. She hadn't intended to bring up the apparition.

Laurie was startled. "What? The woman in white made an appearance?"

"She did—and scared the panties off the Devils cheerleaders."

"The Devils cheerleaders? *They* saw her?"

"Oh, yes. That kid George from our science class saw to it—him and his cronies."

"I don't get it," Laurie said.

"The Boo Babe is a hoax," Deal explained. "A good one—I have to admit she made a couple of my hairs stand on end, too, when I saw her—but still a hoax. Done with lights and tape recorders and scrim."

"You saw the ghost last night, too?"

"No, not last night. It was last week sometime." She didn't mention the voice that said her name last night. *Delia. Oh, Delia.* How had they done that? How'd they

126

know she'd be around? And why her? *De-li-a.* That voice. It had sounded so real. As if it knew her.

"When was it that you saw her last week? What day?" Laurie asked curiously.

"Wednesday, I think." She pretended to be unsure. "Sometime around five o'clock. I left my pack in school and went back to get it."

"Wednesday? Really? Interesting. Al Benson was edgy when he came over that night."

"Mr. Benson? Do you hang out with him or something?" she asked sharply.

"No, my dad does. Wednesday is their bowling night. Did you see him that day? Did he let you into the school?"

She hesitated, uncomfortable. "He let me *out.* He . . . guessed I'd seen something. I didn't tell him about it. Which was just as well since the hoax was aimed at him."

"How do you know that?"

"Let's just say I have my sources."

"Hmm . . ." Laurie was silent for a moment. Then he said, "You're sure it was George and his friends?"

"Pretty sure. Why?" Deal asked.

"Because at five o'clock on Wednesday I delivered a pizza to George's house for him and his buddies."

"Oh. Well, maybe it wasn't Wednesday." Deal kept her voice nonchalant.

"Or maybe . . ." He paused. ". . . it wasn't George."

"Right," she said calmly. But her mind was whirling. If not George last Wednesday, then who? Carter, all by himself? That didn't seem possible. And who was that in the music room last night, calling her name? Certainly not Carter—he'd been in the corridor with Mark. Had George and his friends stayed there, hiding, while she and Mark kissed? That didn't make any sense. Unable to think of an answer, she glanced down at her hands. They were clenched. She opened them slowly, carefully, hoping Laurie hadn't noticed the crescent-shaped marks her nails had dug into her palms.

chapter fifteen

"Maybe you should stay home today," Deal said over Tuesday-morning breakfast, which for her was a cup of coffee and leftover rice from Saturday night's Chinese food.

"Nonsense," said Gram. She had done little but sleep for the past two days, her days off, but she still looked pale and sounded hoarse. "There are people a lot sicker than I am who need their medication."

"Let Mr. Fiorello take care of them," Deal said. Mr. Fiorello, the owner, was in his seventies and worked just two days a week now.

"Nonsense," Gram repeated. And that was that.

Deal felt a bit sick herself as she headed for school. Several nights of poor sleep hadn't helped. With hard and constant effort she'd managed to keep thoughts of ghosts and hoaxes at bay during the daytime. But at night, they ran amok in her dreams.

It had taken all her concentration and a full class of

noisy and very corporeal students to get her into home-room. She sat pulling her sweater tightly around her, her hands tucked under her armpits. "You coming down with something?" Laurie asked. "Vitamin C's good if you're catching a cold."

"I'm fine," she replied.

"Garlic and honey are good, too," he offered. "They'll protect your throat—"

"I'm *fine*," Deal snapped.

"Okay, okay," he backed off.

She was glad. She couldn't cope with his solicitousness today. She was also pleased they had no rehearsal after school, so she could avoid him—and Room 513.

She coasted through the morning, only half-listening to the discussions and conversations going on around her until lunchtime. She'd finished her rather wilted salad and was doodling on a napkin while the Sun King's court twittered over the upcoming Valentine's Day dance.

"Who are you going with, Deal?" asked Tina.

"Yeah. Who *are* you going with?" Carter smirked. He'd been smirking since Saturday night. It annoyed her. She needed to put a stop to it.

"You," she said.

"Whoa!" "All right!" "Huh-huh-huh!" came the taunts and whistles from around the table.

"You are free, aren't you?" she said.

"Yeah. Yeah, I'm free. Free and easy," Carter said, smirking again.

Deal swore silently, Damn, what did I just do? She glanced at Mark. He was smiling with narrowed eyes. Jean's eyes were even narrower, and there wasn't the trace of a smile on her face.

Well, well, well. Look at that, said the voice in Deal's head. *A double whammy. You should be proud of yourself.*

Oh, yeah. Real proud. Her throat felt scratchy, as though she'd swallowed a fish bone.

The bell rang. She gathered up her tray. The napkin she'd been doodling on fluttered off. She bent and picked it up. She'd drawn a picture of a coffin. Across the lid she'd written the name "Marie." She crumpled it quickly before anyone could notice.

She thought about telling Carter it had been a joke, that she had another date for the dance or that she had another dance to go to elsewhere. She thought of forfeiting the whole Game. I could quit it. Just like that, she told herself. But she couldn't, and she knew it.

Right before gym, Tina pulled her aside and said, "I know you didn't mean to, but you got Jean upset. She was hoping Carter would ask her to the dance."

"She never mentioned that she liked Carter," Deal said.

"Well, not to *you*. But everybody else knows."

"Including Carter?"

"Especially Carter . . . He's been kind of playing a game with her."

"Then what does she want him for?"

"You know how it is. You can't help who you like," Tina said.

"*I* can." Deal hadn't meant to say that aloud.

Tina cocked her head. "Really? And you *like* Carter?"

Deal didn't reply immediately. "Sure," she said at last. "I like him."

"But he's not Mr. Big Night, is he?"

Let it go, Deal. Now's your chance to let the whole thing go, she thought. But she just let Tina go on.

"Look, what I'm trying to say is why not let Carter go to the dance with Jean? There must be someone else you'd like to go with or, if he's unavailable, I could help fix you up with somebody. . . . Like Adam, from History. He's so nice. And he doesn't have a date. Or Bob. You and Bob would make a great couple. I can see you both in dark blue. . . ."

Who does she think she is, the Angel of Mercy? said the dry voice. *Trying to help poor loveless little Deal. Just like Mommy when she used to invite kids over to be your friends?*

Damn it. Damn *you*, Deal snarled. "Maybe I will go with someone else to the dance, Tina," she said with a smile.

"Oh, good. Let me know when you want my help."

"I'll do that," Deal said.

The late bell rang. "Oops," said Tina. "We'd better hurry. You know Ms. Maraldi."

"Yes. Could you tell her I'm in the girls' room with cramps?" Deal pressed her stomach.

"Oh, you poor thing," said Tina. "Sure, I'll tell her."

Deal waited till the locker room had emptied. Then she took out a piece of paper. On it she wrote, "How about that ride? Kerrit Park, 8:00." She ran lightly down to the doorway and looked out. The coast was clear.

Mark's locker was conveniently near the music room. Deal had made it a point to know exactly which one it was. She darted to it and slipped the note through the vents.

The King's in check, said the voice in her head.

Yeah, she replied. And the Queen doesn't even know it. She rubbed her stomach. It had started to hurt for real.

"I hope you like roast beef," Carolyn said. "I'm not a cucumber sandwich girl myself."

"Yes, I do," said Deal. She was sitting in Carolyn's kitchen with August on her lap. Carolyn had called her as soon as Deal got home. She'd found the yearbook at last. She invited Deal to see it and join her for tea.

"Good. Because if you don't mind my saying so, you look as though you could use a good meal. I'm very fond of your grandmother, but I know that cooking's not her forte." She set a platter in front of Deal, who dug in without hesitating. The food was good—and Deal knew she wouldn't get to see the photos until she finished every last bite.

"So, how is your mother doing in . . . Minnesota, is it?"

Deal didn't correct her. She didn't want to talk about her mother. "She's fine," she said. Or maybe she wasn't. There'd been a letter—a long, rambling letter, complaining about her job and Clark's job and the weather. "Call you soon," she'd signed off. The honeymoon is over—sooner than I expected, Deal thought, realizing that she didn't feel any glee over it. If Renee wanted her back, would she go? Last week she would have said yes. Now she wasn't so sure.

"Do you like her boyfriend?" Carolyn asked.

He's all right, Deal was about to say. But the food, the cozy kitchen, and Carolyn's kind gaze lulled her into telling the truth. "Not much," she replied.

Carolyn smiled sympathetically and reached for another slice of meat. Deal noticed that she ate with relish, but also grace—the same grace Mark had. "You know, I met your father once," Carolyn said after a pause.

Deal's heart gave an extra thump. No one she knew ever mentioned her father, much less had met him. "You did?" she said.

"Yes. Your parents were moving to Redland. They stopped to visit. Your mother was pregnant with you. They were both so attractive. Everyone said so at the Labor Day picnic. The Roland Street Merchants Association held it every year—still does. It's a real old-fashioned affair—lots of food and games, especially races. . . ." She paused as though she was about to say something and thought better of it. "They had a good time. Your dad was the life of the party."

"I bet he bet on every one of those races," Deal blurted.

"Well, yes, actually. He did," Carolyn admitted.

Deal laughed humorlessly. She felt deeply disappointed. Her knowledge about her father was pitifully scant. She'd been hoping Carolyn could tell her something she didn't know.

Then Carolyn said, "He also sang to you."

"To me? I thought you said Renee—my mother was still pregnant."

"She was. He sang to her belly. He said he was sure you could hear him. He wanted you to grow up musical, like him. He had a gorgeous voice."

"He did?" Deal said. She felt breathless. No one had told her that before. It was a gift.

"Yes. And he was very gentle with your mom, massaging her back and feet. Half the women there fell in love with him—myself included. The interesting thing is he didn't seem to know it—which made him all the more charming."

Deal swallowed down the lump in her throat. "Thank you," she said softly.

Carolyn smiled. Then she laughed. "I just remembered. My daughter-in-law was pregnant, too—with Mark. Your father tried to get my son to sing to *her* belly. The only problem is Mark senior sounds like a foghorn. And now Mark junior does as well."

Deal smiled down at her fork.

"Well, I expect you'd like to see those pictures now," Carolyn said.

"Oh, yes. I would," said Deal. She'd nearly forgotten about them.

Carolyn got up and returned swiftly with a red bound book and a small stack of photos. "Let me show you my family first. Here they are. My daughter Linda, the pregnant one, is due in a month. Sam and I will be going to her house to help out. I thought you could take care of August then."

"Fine," said Deal.

"Wonderful. Now here's the same crew ten years ago visiting me at the pharmacy. There's your grandmother and Mr. Fiorillo in the picture."

Backward in time she went. More group shots at the store, the oldest from twenty-five years ago when Gram had started working there. She didn't look very different—a bit less gray and lined, perhaps. Her straight posture and unsmiling face varied little from photo to photo.

"She looks the same," Deal said aloud.

"Yes, she does," Carolyn said.

"Did she act the same, too, twenty-five years ago?"

"Pretty much."

"I heard she was different in high school."

"Yes, she was. I didn't know her well then. But I thought she was very sophisticated. She had a lot of boyfriends. I think some of the girls were . . . well . . ."

"Envious of her?" Deal suggested.

"That—and afraid of her, too. She got what she wanted." Carolyn opened the yearbook and began turning the pages.

Deal glanced over her shoulder at the array of faces, smooth, spotty, dark, fair, many hopeful, most unaware, all with their activities and a suitable quote printed below their names. "Here she is," said Carolyn.

Deal stared down at the picture. The short dark hair. The half-smile. The teasing gaze. "Maureen D. Murray," it said beneath. "She walks in beauty like the night . . ." Deal was looking at a Gram she never knew. She was looking at herself. Like grandmother, like granddaughter. How much am I like Gram? How many traits besides looks got passed from one generation to another? Deal didn't like thinking about those questions.

"Are there other pictures of her in here?" she asked after a moment.

"A few. Have a look."

While Carolyn fixed tea and dessert, Deal leafed slowly through the yearbook. There was Gram at the homecoming dance, smiling in the arms of a cute, fair-haired boy; at a basketball game, cheering in the stands; and at the ice rink, clowning with a pretty, dimpled, long-haired girl. But that was all—no pictures of her at the prom or on the class trip.

Deal reached the last page of the book. On it was a head shot of the same dimpled girl from the photo with Gram. Underneath her picture were the words "IN MEMORIAM. Marie Scarpetti. 1933–1950." Deal's chest ached. She pressed her hand against it.

"Poor Marie," Carolyn said, setting down Deal's tea. "She was hit by a car over by Ratched Road."

"Yes," Deal replied, still staring at the photo. "I know."

"It happened the night of the Valentine's Day dance. Very sad. She and your grandmother were friends for a while."

"Did they have a falling-out?" Deal asked carefully.

"I don't really know," Carolyn answered. "I know that Marie and her boyfriend Tony did. Tony Benson, now there was a handsome guy. He went off to college in California and never moved back here. He became a doctor out there, I think." She flipped to his photo. He *was* handsome, with dark hair and a serious smile. The type of guy Deal knew she would have chosen some forty years ago.

"Benson? He's not related to the jan—the custodian, is he?"

"Oh, yes. Al's his brother. They used to say Tony got all the looks, brains, and talent in the family. Al got what was left. . . . Oh, dear. Forget I said that. It wasn't kind or even true. Al Benson is a very nice man."

The phone rang then. Carolyn went to answer it. Deal was grateful for the moment alone. Questions roiled and tumbled in her head. Faces swam before her eyes—Marie and Tony fixed in time, Gram and Mr. Benson the way they looked and acted today. There was something about them all that tugged at her. Some pattern she could almost see.

Carolyn returned, agitated. "That was my son-in-law," she said. "My daughter's gone into premature labor. We'll have to leave as soon as Frank gets home from work. . . . I'll leave instructions for you about August." She opened a cabinet. "Here's a key." Deal stood up to go. "You don't have to rush, dear. Finish your tea while I make some calls. . . . I've enjoyed your visit. You have to come again." She left the room.

Deal stood there for a moment, looking after her, then

down at the yearbook. She'd never seen a copy of it at Gram's. She wondered if it was something else her grandmother had hidden away. "Thanks for lunch, and other things," she told Carolyn on her way out the door. But she didn't think the woman heard her.

chapter sixteen

D eal was late. *Let* him *wait this time,* the voice in her head had said, and Deal told herself she was just following instructions.

The truth was she wasn't so sure she wanted to go through with it. All during the movie she'd gone to (and hardly watched), she'd tried to get in the right mood for seeing Mark, the dark, dangerous mood that had led her to make the date in the first place. Instead, she felt sad and confused—a gambler who suspects that all her winnings won't pay for what she's lost.

She sat on a bench at the stop, letting two buses go by before she boarded the third, which dropped her off next to Kerrit Park.

Near the entrance the streetlight glinted off the chrome on his bike. He stepped out of the shadows, impatiently swinging the extra helmet in his hand, and looked up the street. She wondered how many times he'd made Tina wait. I'm avenging you, Tina, she told herself, knowing that was absurd.

"Mark," she called to him in a low voice.

He whipped around so quickly that he stumbled. His one rare instance of clumsiness made her think of Laurie. She reached out and caught him.

He righted himself quickly. "I thought maybe you'd changed your mind," he said.

"Why? Have you?" she asked.

She expected him to laugh or hand her another line. Instead, soberly, he said, "I almost did."

She didn't respond.

"Why are you going to the dance with Carter?" Mark asked.

"Why not?" she said.

"You know why not."

"Would you rather I stayed home?"

"Of course not."

"What, then?"

In answer, he handed her the helmet and straddled the bike. "Get on," he said.

Deal stood there, not wanting to obey him too quickly. Then slowly she slid onto the seat.

He handled the bike well, purring down the park's winding paths, gliding smoothly over the snowy patches, avoiding the icy ones. It was a little more tame than Deal liked—and a lot more cold. But still it felt good—the stinging wind, the warmth of Mark's back against her chest, the whiteness and silence of the park.

When Mark stopped at the old stables, closed for the season, her lips were so numb that she barely felt his kisses. It didn't matter. She was happy again—at the top of her game. She pulled off his helmet and tossed it away. He tackled her then and they tussled in the snow. She let him pin her.

"Swear!" he demanded, imitating Hamlet's father's ghost.

"Swear what?" she panted.

"Swear you won't go to the dance with Carter. Swear you'll tell him it was just a joke."

"I swear!" she declared. "I won't go to the dance with Carter—if I go with you."

He released her and stood up. "I can't do that," he said.

She rose. "We'd better go." Her voice was as cold as the snow she was brushing off her coat.

He retrieved his helmet from a bush. When he tried to kiss her again, she pulled away. "Look, I want to be with you. But I can't dump Tina like that. Believe it or not, I'm actually not that kind of guy," he said, his tone both wry and pleading. "You're the only girl besides Tina I've liked this way. I don't even know why I like you. I know you're playing with me. But it's like I can't stop myself."

She could tell it was the truth. What are you doing,

Deal, and why are you doing it? she asked herself. The same distaste and guilt she'd felt earlier washed over her.

"We really have to go," she said, more plainly now. She shivered.

"You're cold. You have to dress warmer next time." He took off his scarf and wrapped it gallantly around her neck.

"At least I wore gloves," she said with a faint laugh that Mark misunderstood, and she pulled the scarf up to cover her nose and mouth.

They got on the bike. He retraced their trail through the park and out into town. At a stoplight, he said, "I have to bring the bike to the mall. My brother manages the movie theater there—he'll be getting off work soon. I'll drop you at my car while I return his keys so you don't have to wait in the cold."

And so nobody sees us together, Deal thought.

His car was in the employees', not customers', lot. She almost laughed at his extra precautions. She slipped off the bike, looped the scarf around his neck, and held out her hand for the car key.

He reached into his pocket, but his hand froze. He swore under his breath.

"What is it?" she asked, turning.

Coming out of the back exit of Mr. Chocolate, where he worked, was Mitch Jefferson. Which didn't matter at all. What did matter—very much indeed—was that Jean Herrick was with him, looking their way with scorn.

chapter seventeen

———————

"You came in late last night," Gram said. Her skin looked almost translucent, except for the big dark circles under her eyes. Instead of her usual ramrod posture, she sat slightly hunched, holding tightly to her mug of morning coffee as if she was afraid she might drop it.

"No, I didn't. You went to bed early," Deal, who suspected she didn't look a whole lot better, replied. It was true. She'd been in by ten. Mitch, who lived nearby, had driven her and Jean home. Deal doubted that they believed Mark's story about the two of them running into each other in the parking lot and Mark offering her a ride. Part of her didn't care whether they did or not.

Gram let out a sound that might have been a humph or else a snuffle. Then she shivered.

"Are you cold?" Deal asked.

"A little," Gram admitted.

Deal started to reach across the table to feel Gram's

forehead the way Renee always felt hers whenever she was ill. But she quickly thought better of it. "Do you have a fever?" she asked instead.

"I don't know. Maybe a slight one."

"You mean you haven't taken your temperature yet?"

"Are you my doctor?" Gram said petulantly.

"Have you called her?" Deal answered back.

"I will if I need to. I know my own body, thank you."

Yeah, you know it—and you're afraid of it. It was a thought Deal had never quite formed before. The stiff posture, the soldierly gait, the iron gray hair screwed into a twist or a bun—they were all signs of someone who was scared of her body, of what it might do if she didn't keep it under tight control.

But she hadn't always been like that. Deal had the proof right in her backpack.

Gram rose and staggered—not much, but enough to make her steady herself on the back of her chair.

"Gram, please stay home today," Deal said with real concern.

"We went through this yesterday. I told you I'm all right—and I'm going to work." She marched out of the room, taking care not to wobble.

Jean had told. That was clear from the chill between Mark and Tina that threatened to cover the whole home-room with frost.

"What's going on over there?" Laurie asked when Deal took her seat.

"Why ask me?" she answered tightly.

"I thought I would go to the source."

Deal didn't flinch under the accusation—nor did she deny it.

Frowning, Laurie opened his copy of *Hamlet*.

Deal watched him quietly for a moment. There was a fleck of red glitter in his hair—the kind you'd find on party hats or valentines. "Laurie . . ." she began.

He turned to her.

Laurie, what? Laurie, help me? Laurie, tell me how to stop playing the Game? "Are you going to the Valentine's Day dance?" she finished.

He was surprised by the question. "I'm supposed to work," he said cautiously.

"Oh, right."

"Although," he went on, "I suspect Louie, my boss, might let me have the night off if I polished his floor with my kneecaps." He waited for her to respond. When she didn't, he asked, "Are you going?"

"I don't know," she replied.

Again, he waited. Deal knew why. *He's expecting me to ask him to the dance. My fault. I shouldn't have let him think I was going to,* she told herself. *What a ridiculous idea—me and that clown. That kid.* But she remembered how he was the other day. *Not a clown. Certainly* not a kid. An image floated into her head of the two of them slow dancing. He'd sing into her hair and smell like apples. And she'd feel *real* in his arms. Real? She scoffed at herself. What is that, Deal? Do you know? Will you *ever* know?

She turned and stared at Mark. He glanced at her and looked away.

"Did you ever dream you're riding down a highway, and you know it goes nowhere, but you can't get off because you can't find the exit?" she murmured.

"What?" Laurie asked. "What did you say?"

"Nothing," she replied.

She didn't feel like having lunch with them. She spent the time instead in the library, her head on the table, sleeping. In gym she got as far as the locker room, where she saw Tina, eyes puffy, cheeks mascara-stained, before she turned and hurried out toward the girls' room—not the gym girls' room, full of nosy classmates, but the one the smokers, unconcerned with anything but their butts, used.

She never got there. Carter stopped her in the hall. He didn't mince words. "We still going to the dance?" he asked.

Deal, too, decided to be direct. "I don't think so," she said.

He nodded. "Okay. But let me give you a tip. If you're

counting on Mark, don't. Tina's been around longer than you have."

"Thanks for the advice," Deal said coldly.

"You're welcome."

Then the Sun King himself appeared, and Carter faded.

"You weren't at lunch," Mark said.

"No," Deal agreed.

"Tina and I had a fight."

"So I gathered."

"That witch Jean told her. I don't know what she was angrier about—that I was with you or that I was riding the bike. I told her I don't need her telling me what to do."

"What *do* you need?" Deal asked.

"You," he said. "I need you. . . . Granca gave you a key to her house, right?"

"Yes," she said.

"Let's go there after practice."

Deal hesitated.

What are you waiting for? said the voice in her head. *This is it. Checkmate.*

I hate this game, Deal answered. I hate you.

"Say yes," Mark said. "Please say yes."

"Yes," said Deal.

He pushed her back against a locker, kissing her hard, there in the hall, not caring who was looking. Then he left. She watched him peel away. Never before had she felt so victorious. Or so doomed.

She cut the rest of her classes and hung out at a nearby coffee shop, reading a book about angels, eating greasy french fries, drinking cups of coffee heavy with sugar and milk. The waitress kept giving her disapproving looks, but since the place was nearly empty and Deal kept ordering, there was nothing she could say.

She got back to school ten minutes before her last class ended and headed for Room 513. She told herself she might as well go to rehearsal, and then exit, gloriously, on Mark's arm. But she knew that wasn't it—not all of it. French, math, history, they were all disposable. But the duet was not.

The music room was dark and empty when she got there. The blinds were open, but the day was so dull and gray that little light penetrated the room. She put her hand on the doorknob and held it there. It had been hard enough going inside this morning, even with a full and noisy class. But now it felt almost impossible. She let go of the knob. What if she left now? Maybe she *could* live without the duet. She took a step back, then stopped. No, you can't give in, she told herself. You do, and you really are a loser. She stepped forward, opened the door, and strode inside.

Immediately, she reached for the light switch. Uh-uh, she told herself. Don't turn it on. This will be a test. If you can stand here for ten minutes without freaking out, you pass—and you'll never have to worry about taking it again.

She crossed to the center of the room next to the piano and stood facing the blackboard, breathing slowly in and out, in and out. Her shoulders were hunched. She forced them to relax. It was so quiet she could hear the clock clicking off the seconds. Two minutes went by. Five. Soon she'd be home free.

Suddenly the room went cold. Colder than Kerrit Park last night. Colder than a morgue. A shape appeared, and even though it was unformed, Deal could recognize it—but was no less frightened by its familiarity. "Oh, God," she gasped, shaking.

The shape became clearer, so clear this time that Deal could see its face—a young, pretty face, but sad and reproachful, the face she'd seen in the yearbook. "Delia," it said. "Oh, Delia."

"Wh-what do you w-want?" Deal stammered.

"Delia," it said and began to advance.

"Leave me alone! Leave me alone!" she begged in a hoarse whisper.

"Delia." The ghost stretched out wispy hands.

Delia tried to scream, but couldn't make a sound.

Then it vanished.

Deal sank to her knees.

That was how Laurie and Mr. Ferrara found her.

"You're not by any chance praying, are you, Delia?" Mr. Ferrara said, with thinly disguised sarcasm.

But Laurie helped her up. "What is it?" he said. "What happened?"

In answer she wrenched herself from his grasp and fled the school.

chapter eighteen

"I called the doctor. She's coming here at four o'clock," Gram said. She was standing at the foot of Deal's bed.

Deal had spent most of the past two days in it, avoiding all social contacts, even phone calls—except for one. She'd been on her way to the bathroom when she heard Renee's voice pour into the answering machine.

"Deal, this is your stupid mother. I am so sorry I haven't called and so sorry that I left you with Gram. What you must think of me . . . I hope you can forgive me because—"

It was then Deal picked up the phone. "Because what?" she'd asked. She wanted to sound detached, unaffected. She didn't want the phone call to matter as much as it did.

"Deal! You're there! Why are you there? Why aren't you in school? Are you sick?"

"A little," Deal said.

"What is it? A cold?"

It's a cold, all right. Colder than the grave, she nearly said, and suddenly she ached to tell her mother the truth.

But Renee was already barreling on, "Oh, you poor baby. I am, too. Sick with missing you."

How corny, how fake, Deal thought. But still she felt her heart squeeze and her eyes sting. She's got me. Like always.

"Do you miss me?"

Deal nodded, then, realizing her mother couldn't hear that, whispered, "Yes."

"Well, you won't have to much longer. We're going to be together again."

It should have been loving, warm, but the statement felt jagged. "Why?" she asked, snagged.

"Because I'm leaving Clark!" Renee announced and began to rail against him in a garbled mixture of fury, self-pity, and yearning.

Deal agreed with everything bad she said about Clark, but when she told Renee so, her mother began to defend him, so Deal soon said nothing. When Renee stopped talking at last, both of them were exhausted.

"So, when are you coming?" Deal asked after letting Renee catch her breath.

"Coming for what?"

Deal wondered if her mother's long tirade was like

some self-erasing tape—play it once and it's gone, leaving no trace behind. "For me," she reminded.

"Oh. Soon. Soon!" Renee had declared. "I promise. . . . Oh, my God, look at the time. . . . I've used up my whole break. . . . My darling, please take care of that cold. . . . I love you." And she'd hung up.

Deal hadn't mentioned the call to Gram—she knew what Gram would say and she didn't want to hear it.

"I don't need a doctor," she told Gram now. "*You* haven't seen a doctor."

"I don't need to see her. You do."

"Why? I'm not any sicker than you are."

"Then get up and go to school."

When Deal didn't answer, Gram wearily looked at the clock. "My lunch break's almost over. Can I get you anything before I go?"

Deal shook her head.

"Okay, then. Four o'clock," Gram reminded and left.

Deal pulled the covers up to her chin and lay there, staring at the ceiling. I could stay here forever, she thought. She felt like one of those Victorian ladies who retreated to their beds with nervous disorders, their bodies dissolving into their sagging mattresses. She wondered if any of them had ever confessed to seeing a ghost. She wondered if any doctor would have believed them if they had. She knew none would believe her.

She closed her eyes and fell into a doze, too light for whole dreams, but deep enough for fragments—a feast of pregnant picnickers in a park; a lonely girl walking in the snow; an oncoming car, swerving to avoid a cat.

She sat up in bed, twitching. August! Oh, my God. I haven't fed the cat! She looked at the clock. Three-fifteen. If she hurried, she wouldn't run into the doctor. She got out of bed, threw on some clothes, and rushed toward the door, but a wave of dizziness hit her and she had to sit down right in the middle of the hall. Her head between her knees, she realized that not only hadn't August eaten for two days, but neither had she.

She managed to get up and go to the kitchen, where she gobbled two rolls and drank a Coke so quickly she almost threw up. She had to breathe steadily until her stomach settled down. She glanced at the clock there. Three forty-five. Get out of here, Deal. She loped to the door.

The bell rang just as she got there. Damn! The doctor *would* have to be early. She peered through the peep-hole. The figure on the porch wasn't a doctor. It was Laurie.

Why is he here? I didn't ask him to come. And I don't want to see him. I don't want to see anybody. She thought about waiting till he left. But the doctor was bound to show up by then and she'd have to wait for her to go, too, while poor August felt hungrier and more abandoned by the minute.

She took a deep breath and opened the door.

"Deal! Thank God you're okay. You scared the—"

"I don't have time to talk, Laurie." She took off down the street.

He followed. "What happened? Your grandmother—did she tell you I called?—said you were sick. But the other day you looked . . . terrified."

She moved faster, trying to shake him. But she knew by now it was impossible. As the bus pulled up to the stop, she turned to him. "Come or go, Laurie. But either way, shut up." She got on the bus.

He got on with her, silently. All the way to Carolyn's she worried about the cat, picturing her emaciated, dehydrated, or worse—guilt making her unreasonable because it had, after all, only been two days.

When the bus stopped, she was out the doors while they were still opening. She sprinted to the house, not even glancing at Laurie, and fumbled with the lock.

August, mewing pitifully and fatter than ever, was waiting for her.

"You poor thing," Deal said, scooping her up and carrying her to the kitchen. A ripped bag of kibble lay on the floor, next to the cabinet August had managed to pry open. Deal took one look and began to laugh—loud, wild guffaws booming out of her like cannonballs. She couldn't stop them.

Then she began to quiver. She could feel the hot tears welling and she tried to force them back. Her body shook with the effort.

Then Laurie put his hand on her back and she couldn't stop them any longer. She wept while he held her. He kept holding her even after she stopped crying and began to talk, both of them sitting on the kitchen floor, Laurie's back against the refrigerator, Deal's back against his chest so she didn't have to look at him.

"She thought I wouldn't be there. She thought she'd be talking to the answering machine," she said.

"Who?" Laurie asked gently.

"My mother. She called when she expected me to be in school. And she's such a liar. She doesn't miss me. I'm not the man in her life. I'm only her daughter."

"That stinks, Deal," Laurie declared.

When he didn't try to soften his statement with glib words of assurance, she trusted him enough to say, "There's more, Laurie."

"Do you want to tell me the rest?"

"Yes," she said, and she poured out the story of the ghost, the valentine, the pattern she was trying to piece together.

"You think the ghost is Marie Scarpetti," he said when at last she'd finished.

Deal gave a half nod, then blurted, "Oh God, I can't believe I'm talking about this, making it real."

"It *is* real," Laurie replied. He couldn't quite hide the tinge of excitement in his voice.

She decided to forgive him for it. "What if it isn't?" she said, her voice so shrunken it scared her.

"You mean what if you're going crazy?"

"Yes."

"No way. Al Benson isn't crazy and neither are you," he said, with such conviction she had to believe him.

After a moment, she said, "But why *did* she appear to us—to *me*? She called me, Laurie. She called my *name*." She shuddered.

He rubbed her arms slowly, trying to smooth away the goose bumps. "Do you really want to find out?"

The question loomed like a doorway. She didn't know what was on the other side, but she felt that going through it would change her life and quite possibly her soul. She wanted that more than anything in the world and she didn't want it at all.

Deal pulled away from Laurie and busied herself with filling August's water dish, putting away the torn bag of cat food, and sweeping up the scattered bits. Then she went to the bathroom and changed the litter. When she returned to the kitchen, Laurie was still by the fridge, standing now. She thought maybe he'd have gone. Or maybe she'd wished it. But that was an old game—and Laurie never had, never would play it.

"Yes. I want to find out," she said.

"I'll go with you," he said.

She nodded. She picked up August and cuddled her briefly. "I'll be back tomorrow," she swore into her fur. She'd wear that oath like an amulet for protection against whatever was about to come.

chapter nineteen

D eal's hand hovered over the buzzer. Laurie stood a little behind her, giving her space. Fear—such a new companion—pricked her in a dozen places. She rang the bell.

It took a long time for Mr. Benson to appear—so long that Deal almost turned to go. But then she heard the click of the lock and the school door opened.

"I . . . we left something," Deal said, expecting him to say, "Again?"

He looked at her keenly. "In room five-thirteen?"

"Yes."

"This way," he said, as if they were strangers and needed directions.

"We can find it by ourselves."

"Maybe you can—and maybe you can't," Mr. Benson said.

There was no use arguing, Deal knew. And besides, for better or worse, Al Benson had a right to be there. He was part of the pattern, too. She and Laurie fell into step behind him as he led them to the music room.

The custodian unlocked the door and all three entered. The room was stuffy. It smelled like chalk dust and Cheetos—familiar, normal smells. Nobody turned on the lights.

I am crazy, Deal thought. Or, at least, this is. She stood next to Laurie—not touching him, but close enough for the hair on her arms to prickle from his electricity. He was humming their duet—so quietly Deal wasn't sure whether or not she heard or merely felt it. "Someday my happy arms will hold you . . ." it went. She thought about the night she was in this room with Mark. His arms, his hard kisses. She felt a twinge of regret. I had him, she thought. *You could have him still,* the voice in her head whispered faintly. For the briefest of moments she let herself listen to it.

And all at once she felt the already familiar cold. Laurie stopped humming and reached for her hand. His was big and surprisingly warm. She gripped it as if it was the only thing keeping her upright. The hazy shape formed before them, its features clearer than ever.

"Oh, Delia," it admonished.

Laurie breathed in sharply.

"So it is her," Mr. Benson rasped.

Deal, willing her voice steady, said, "What do you want, Marie?"

The ghost moved its lips, but no sound came out. It

raised one hand to its head as if trying to remember how to put together more than two words. When it spoke at last, its voice was as thin and pale as its face. "The heart. I want the heart."

"The heart? You mean the valentine, don't you?" Deal said.

"Oh, Delia. The heart . . ."

"Why do you want it back? You gave it to Gram, didn't you?"

"You took the heart."

"I didn't take anything," Deal insisted. "All I did was look at it."

"You took the heart," the ghost repeated. And as if the strain of speaking was too much, it began to fade.

"Wait. Don't go! I'm telling you, the valentine's still there. In Gram's closet . . ."

"Oh, Delia," the ghost murmured, and was gone.

"No! Wait! What does she want? Why does she keep calling me?" With sudden fury, Deal banged on the piano so hard that Laurie grabbed her hands.

When the jangling subsided, Mr. Benson said quietly, "I don't think it's you she wants." He opened the blinds and the moonlight poured in.

Still angry, Deal whirled on him. "What do you mean?"

"I didn't see the resemblance before, but now I do. She's calling your grandmother."

"But my grandmother's name is Maureen."

"Now it is. But years ago she went by Delia. It's her middle name, isn't it?"

"That's right," Deal murmured. "It is."

And suddenly all the pieces came together. "Tony and Marie had a fight," she said to the custodian. "They never made up."

Mr. Benson nodded. "Tony thought she'd forgive him, but she never did."

"Oh yes she did. Only he never knew it. And then, the night she died, he took another girl to the Valentine's dance, didn't he? He took Delia Murray."

"That's right."

"Oh, God," Deal sighed. Like grandmother, like granddaughter.

"So, you see, Marie wasn't calling you after all," said the custodian.

Deal looked at Laurie. She knew he understood. "Yes, she was, Mr. Benson," she said softly. "She was."

chapter twenty

———————

"Well, how nice of you to come back—and with company," Gram said. She was sitting in a chair by the living room window. Every light was on, making the quiet room seem noisy.

"This is Laurie," Deal said. "You already know Mr. Benson."

"Hello, Ms. Murray," Laurie greeted.

"Hello, Delia," the custodian said, sitting on the sofa.

She winced at the name, then glared at Deal. "There's been a lot of company today. Mark Chelsom was here looking for you. On his motorcycle. He seemed upset about something. Perhaps you know what it was."

Ignoring her sardonic tone, Deal consciously chose to sit on the hassock at Gram's feet. It was as close as she could get to her grandmother without touching her. "Gram," she said, "we have to talk about Marie Scarpetti."

"You have been poking around, haven't you?" Gram tried to sound sharp, but her voice had gone brittle.

"She's the Brain Rot ghost," Deal said.

"Please! I've told you—there are no such things as ghosts."

"There are, Gram. I didn't want to believe in them, either. But they exist. At least, Marie does. I saw her, and so did they. She wants the valentine back. The one she sent to Tony. The one you took."

Gram closed her eyes and pressed her fingers hard against the lids. No one said anything. The only sound in the room was the creak of Laurie's knees as he shifted position. He was still standing, trying to be there in case Deal needed him and not there if she didn't. Deal motioned him to sit. He smiled and shook his head.

A car passed by outside, so quickly it made the windows buzz. Somewhere in the distance, sirens screamed. Then it was quiet again until Gram at last began to speak.

"I don't remember when I first noticed Tony Benson. Maybe after I stopped seeing John. Or was it Carl. Or perhaps Lloyd," she said with self-derision. "I do know when I decided to steal him away from Marie. It was during the Christmas concert when I heard the two of them sing that song. The song you were singing the other day . . ." She nodded at Deal with her eyes still shut.

As if from a distance, Deal heard Laurie shift again. She believed that if she turned around, he—and Mr. Benson, and indeed the whole room—would be blurred like the background of a film when the camera focuses close and sharp on the center of the screen.

"It wasn't easy, getting him. He and Marie were really crazy about each other, always sending love notes. . . . But she wanted to act in the school play and he didn't. Ever the good friend, I encouraged her—and while she was at rehearsals, I encouraged him. . . . They had a fight. Marie had a temper. She said some awful things, then felt really bad. . . . It was almost Valentine's Day, and she decided to apologize in a card. . . . A tasteless card, don't you think?" This time she did look at Deal, pointedly.

"Yes," Deal said.

Gram smiled, acknowledging Deal's admission of guilt and her own. "You're right. I stole it. And Tony, too stubborn to talk to Marie, turned to me. . . . We went to the Valentine's Day dance. I was stunning that night—a picture of glitter and triumph. Tony was dazzled. We danced in the snow, so warm we didn't feel it. . . . And while we were dancing, Marie died." Gram touched her throat. Her face was gray, her eyes clouded with several kinds of pain.

Deal didn't, couldn't move. She was held there, tied to Gram by bonds thin as capillaries, strong as bone.

"I kept the valentine so I wouldn't forget what I'd done," Gram said, her voice so shredded it hurt to hear it. "I stopped seeing Tony and took up with your grandfather. I didn't much like him, so I married him. I thought that would be enough penance. It wasn't . . . You know what they say about the sins of the father—or the mother. . . . Look at Renee. Look at you."

Although Gram's words were hardly a surprise, they still made Deal shudder. Providence or heredity, curse or coincidence? What was this game played out generation after generation? Deal shook her head. Who knows? Whatever it is, it ends now, with me. I can change. I *have* changed. Deal wasn't sure whether or not she'd spoken aloud. She felt suddenly dizzy and gulped air so she wouldn't faint.

But it was Gram who did. Falling off her chair, arms and legs splayed out like a marionette's, skirt rucked up embarrassingly high.

Laurie and Mr. Benson were at her side at once. Laurie discreetly pulled down Gram's skirt, while Mr. Benson felt her pulse. "Call an ambulance!" he barked. But Deal was already halfway to the phone.

It took forever to arrive. By the time it did, Gram was awake, protesting that she didn't need to go to the hospital.

"Gram, be quiet," Deal said. "What took you so long?"

she demanded as the paramedics helped Gram onto a gurney.

"Motorcycle accident," one answered. "Over by Ratched Road."

Deal went cold. "Who? Who was it?" she asked. But she already knew the answer.

chapter twenty-one

D eal took another sip of coffee. Either she'd forgotten how bad it tasted or she was hoping it had somehow improved. It hadn't. She grimaced and set the cup back down just as Tina came into the hospital cafeteria.

Tina saw Deal immediately—which was not surprising since the room wasn't large and there were only two other people in it, strangers because Deal had insisted that Mr. Benson and Laurie go home. Tina hesitated before jutting out her chin and taking a seat opposite Deal.

"Did you see him?" Tina asked bluntly.

"No," said Deal. "I'm here because my grandmother passed out. And they wouldn't let me see him, anyway. Only the immediate family."

"That's right. That's what they said when they wouldn't let me in. I told them I *was* family—or at least I *used* to be." Tina glowered at her.

Deal forced herself to meet Tina's eyes steadily. "I know it's not going to mean much," she said quietly, "but I'm sorry."

"You're right. It doesn't mean much," Tina said.

Deal looked away. The cafeteria manager caught her eye and pointed to the clock. "Closing soon," he called. They were already beginning to stack up the empty chairs. Deal didn't care. She could wait till they booted her out, unlike Renee, who was terrified of being the last customer anywhere.

"The whole school must've seen you and Mark kissing in front of the music room. I guess I was the only one without a front-row seat." More than her anger, Tina's newfound sarcasm bothered Deal. It reminded her too much of herself.

"I really am sorry."

Tina paused, then she blurted, "Why'd you do it? Why'd you go after Mark?"

Deal paused. "Because I could."

"What does that mean?"

"I can't explain. . . ."

"Try," Tina demanded.

Deal took a swallow of the cold, bitter coffee. "They say everybody's supposed to have some talent, something they can do well that makes them feel powerful and strong. Yours is cheerleading. Mine's been catching guys." There was no pride in her voice. But neither was there shame.

171

"Other girls' guys?"

"Sometimes. Not always. But they had to be a challenge. It was a game I played. One I could win." She studied Tina's face. There were two small furrows over the bridge of her nose that Deal hadn't noticed before. Deal could tell that she was trying hard to understand—and couldn't. She wouldn't tell Tina about Gram and Marie. It didn't matter anyway. It didn't change anything.

"Mark loves you, Tina," she said. "He told me so. I . . . I'm quitting the Game. You can have him back."

"How do you know I want him back?" Tina said fiercely. "How do you know he wants me? Don't you think he had something to do with your game? Or do you think you're the only player?"

Deal flinched. First Tina had attacked her for her betrayal, now, changing course, she was trying to strip Deal of her power.

"Don't you think Mark has any mind of his own?" Tina thrust again.

Who knows if he has any mind now at all, Deal thought, with bleak irony. It was clear Tina had just thought the same thing. Her mouth rounded into a small, horrified O. "Oh, God," she said, and began to sob.

Deal didn't weep. She wasn't holding back the tears. She'd cried enough earlier and felt squeezed dry.

The cafeteria manager came over to tell them they had to go. "Leave us alone," they both barked, and he beat a hasty retreat.

They sat there long after Tina stopped crying, neither of them saying another word. They they went downstairs to the waiting room. They sat on sticky plastic chairs, both of them taking turns all night asking about Mark's condition. By morning, it had not changed.

When visiting hours began, Deal, cramped and drained and grateful for a change of scene, went to Gram's room.

Gram was asleep. Her cheeks were slightly flushed like a child's. In fact her whole face looked younger. Deal could trace on it the girl she'd once been.

A nurse came in to fill her water carafe. "How is she?" Deal asked her.

"More tired than she'll admit to," the nurse said, "but otherwise okay. That flu was a nasty sucker."

Deal smiled. Her jaw felt stiff, as if it had gone rusty like the Tin Woodman's. When the nurse left, she sank into the chair next to the bed. Gram's right arm rested on the blanket. Deal reached out and laid her hand palm up in her grandmother's as tenderly as putting a baby in a cradle. Gram stirred slightly but didn't awaken. Deal sat quietly, watching, until her eyes got heavy and she, too, fell asleep.

*   *   *

"Well, just in time for dessert," Gram said when Deal opened her eyes. "Here, have some tapioca. It's so terrible it will make my cooking seem gourmet."

Deal stretched. "What time is it?"

"Twelve-thirty."

Deal yawned. She'd been asleep for over two hours and she didn't feel very rested. Then she remembered why. "Mark," she said and stumbled to her feet.

"What about him?" Gram asked sharply.

Deal told her. "I have to find out if he's . . . how he is."

"I'll come with you," Gram said, pushing away her tray and sliding her feet to the floor.

"No, Gram. You're supposed to rest."

"I've rested enough. If I rest any more, I'll start liking it—and who knows where that might lead," she said, slipping on her robe.

Despite her concern, Deal smiled. That was two jokes Gram had made in the space of two minutes—both about herself. "All right," she conceded. "You can come. I couldn't stop you anyway."

"Damn straight," Gram said.

The moment Deal saw Tina in the waiting room, she knew that Mark was still unconscious. Gram, pulling weight with the nurses she knew, tried to find out more, but there was nothing much to find out.

By late afternoon, when Dr. Pulaski allowed Gram to check out, things still hadn't altered for better or worse.

"I've got to make sure my grandmother gets home okay," Deal said, once again in the waiting room. "Will you call me if anything . . . happens?"

"I don't know," Tina said honestly. She looked faded, like a daffodil pressed in a book.

There was nothing else Deal could say. Then she felt a hand on her shoulder. She turned and looked up at Laurie.

"Hi," she said. "Did you ride your bike here?"

"No, Al Benson drove me." He nodded at the custodian, sitting in a corner of the room with a small bag in his lap.

"Gram's checking out."

"I know. We've come to take her—and you—home."

"You have?" Deal didn't know when her grandmother had talked to Mr. Benson. She was sure Gram hadn't asked him to do her this favor—and was surprised that she'd accepted it at all.

Gram emerged then. Her presence pulled the small group together.

"Free at last," she said. "Or almost." She smiled at Deal, who gave her a puzzled look in return.

"I brought it," Mr. Benson said, handing Gram the bag.

"Thank you . . . I told him where I hide the house key," she explained to Deal, who still didn't understand.

The hospital steps were rimed with a fresh layer of ice.

Without thinking about it, Deal reached for her grandmother's arm to guide her—and Gram let her.

When they got into the car, Deal said, "Could we stop
at Carolyn's house first? I've got to feed August."

"After," Gram said.

"After what?"

Gram handed Deal the bag. She opened it gingerly.
Inside was the small locked metal box. It was time to
return Marie's heart.

chapter twenty-two

They stood in the room for a long time with the box open and the valentine propped inside it like an offering. But the ghost did not appear. Once or twice there was a slight shimmer, a cool breeze, but nothing more. It was gone, like the voice in Deal'shead. Finally, they burned the valentine. It gave off the faint odor of candy and perfume—old pharmacy aromas. Deal wondered if it had come from Fiorillo's, which would have made the circle complete.

" 'Rest, rest, perturbed spirit,' " Laurie quoted. It should have sounded corny, but instead it made Deal's eyes fill with tears.

"Forgive me, Marie," Gram said. Then, after another moment, "We should go."

Deal wanted to stay a little longer. The room felt peaceful now, in a way it never had before.

"We'll meet you in my office," Mr. Benson said. "I'll make your grandmother and myself some coffee."

"Do you think she's really gone?" Laurie asked after the door closed. He was by the piano.

"Yes. I do," Deal said. "Her work is finished."

He played a few notes softly. The opening of "All the Things You Are."

"Go ahead, Laurie," Deal said. "Sing it."

"If you'll sing with me."

"All right." She moved near him and, with perfect timing, they both began, the words and music welling out of them clear, sweet, and strong.

When they finished, Deal took Laurie in her arms and kissed him.

"I might keep trying to get away," she said as he stroked her hair.

"I know."

"Don't let me."

"I won't," he promised.

Holding hands, they walked toward the door.

Before she opened it, Deal turned. "Bye, Marie. And thanks," she murmured.

There was no reply.

"Laurie seems nice," Gram said an hour later when they went into the kitchen.

"Yes, he is." Deal smiled. She glanced at the answering machine. There were three messages. She was afraid to listen to them.

"Whatever it is, you'll want to know," Gram said.

Deal nodded and pressed the play button. "Mark is okay," Tina's voice declared tersely. But Deal could hear the throbbing relief in it. "He's really okay."

"Thank God," Gram said.

Deal shut off the machine, went into the bathroom, and cried. When she came out some time later, she saw that Gram, sitting at the table, hadn't played the other messages yet.

"Go ahead," Gram said, and Deal flicked on the machine again.

The second message was from Renee. "Hi, sweetie. Just wanted to see if you're over your cold. Everything's great here. Clark changed his hours. . . . I'm so happy. . . . Talk to you soon. Love you. Mm-wah!"

What a surprise, Deal thought, with resignation. She had no tears left, and wouldn't have wasted them if she had. She shook her head and avoided Gram's eyes.

The third and final message was from Gram's friend Winston. "Maureen, I'd really like to see you again. Call me."

This time Deal did look at Gram, who had reddened slightly.

"He seems nice, too," Deal said.

"Yes. He is."

"We'll have to learn to deal with nice, won't we?"

"Lord, that'll be a challenge," Gram said wryly.

"Ah, but we both like challenges, don't we?" said Deal.

"Yes," said Gram. "We do."

Deal gave a small smile and rewound the tape.

179

MARILYN SINGER is the author of more than forty books for young readers. Her books for Holt include *It's Hard to Read a Map with a Beagle on Your Lap, Please Don't Squeeze Your Boa, Noah!, Chester the Out-of-Work Dog, The Morgans Dream,* and *A Wasp Is Not a Bee.* Marilyn Singer lives in Brooklyn, New York.